CHEF'S NUTTER HALF

VALE VALLEY SEASON FIVE BOOK 12

ISHA FÁNG

COPYRIGHT

ACKNOWLEDGMENTS

I need to thank bucket loads of people for helping me get this steamy, sizzling story out.

To my family, thank you for leaving me the hell alone when I said I had a deadline to meet.

My sprint partners, thank you for motivating me to write this short in a short time ;).

Sade, you just know how to whip me and get me writing. Amanda, my thesaurus goddess, you rock.

Brooklynn, unmute us.

K.M. Taylor, Britni, ML, thank you for your time.

Maureen, my blurb goddess, you are fantastic. Thank you for helping me on such a short notice.

Angela, thank you for late night sprinting, and helping me fill xxx :D

To my betas—Sabella, Sheryl, Doni, Maggie, and La—thank you for your help and suggestions, and for dealing with my crazy ass questions in the middle of the night.

To my Editor Ann, thank you for polishing my story and turning it into something that is readable :D.

And lastly to my readers. Thank you for taking a chance on my stories and for reading this book.

XoXo
    Isha.

AUTHOR NOTE

This book is one of pure fiction. Any and all characters are based solely on the author's imagination. While researching is used as a base point for the story, it has no standing in fact.

CHAPTER 1

FINNICK

The order bell chimes.

"Order for a plate of paneer korma and two garlic naans," Dina, my head waitress says, sticking the paper on my table.

I frown and glare at the slip of paper, condemning whoever it is that has ordered this.

Why can't people eat the specials mentioned on the board? I'm offering Indian specials today. Chicken tikka, palak paneer, jeera rice, veg pulao, roti, gulab jamun, gajar ka halwa. So many things to choose from.

But no, people want to eat what's not mentioned on the board.

They want to order what's in the menu. Hold the plastic sheet in their hands, flip the pages, browse the names mentioned in them, then contemplate what they want to eat, pick something and then cancel it, check the price, and if it's too pricey, order something else that is cheap and sounds delicious.

So much drama.

I hate drama, especially at the end of the day. It's dark outside, and I have been on my legs for hours.

One more hour to go.

"I can do it," I whisper the words, and fill my lungs with air.

However, that doesn't ease the tension of my body. My body shrinks tighter with tension as I hear noises. Sniggering, coming from the other side of the wall.

Must be the assholes who have ordered this dish.

I think of ways to contaminate his food just for not ordering the specials. I won't do it, but there's no harm in imagining stuff like this.

I hate people.

I really, really hate people.

Thank gods I don't have to interact with them on a daily basis. People get on my nerves, so the less communication I have with them is better for my temper and soul.

I stick the slip on the exhaust fan and remove a pan to prepare paneer korma.

The dish will take 30 mins to prepare.

"Prepare two garlic naans," I tell Clancy, my junior chef.

My kitchen staff is not big. It comprises me, the executive chef. I also act as Chef de Cuisine—a head chef. Then there's Chef de Partie—a station chef—which is Velinda, and Comis Chef—junior chef—which is what Clancy is. And the other two members in my kitchen are Kitchen Porter—Duncan's job, and dishwasher—Eurasia's job.

Oh, and two waitresses.

My diner, The Chef's Corner, is a moderate size restaurant. We only serve lunch and dinner. We cater events as well if we are contacted a month prior to the date.

I want to expand it, build a special VIP floor on top. But, that will mean I have to communicate with contractors and what not to make it happen.

And I do not have—not even a pinch of— the patience to interact with people and listen to them whining.

Just the thought makes me clench my hands into fists, and my body to coil tight with tension.

I hate people.

Frowning, I start the preparation, working silently.

My staff know not to disturb me when I'm in the zone.

This restaurant is my baby. I built it years ago after I arrived at Vale Valley.

It has been more than a decade since I moved here, far away from a place that still haunts me every night.

My family, my babies—

Do not think about them. Just don't.

Absently, I nod and start cutting the onions to make the korma sauce.

My mind... back in focus, somewhat.

Twenty minutes later, Paneer Korma is ready.

So are the garlic naans.

I serve up the dish in a bowl and place it on the tray, then pluck a cilantro and place it on the curry with a roundly sliced carrot.

I ring a bell to let Dina know the dish is ready to be served.

IT'S ALMOST time to close the kitchen. Just another two minutes, and then I can finally sit down.

The image of getting off my feet, propping them on my table in my office, relaxing into my chair, drinking a glass of wine... I silently moan and pray no one wants to meet me or talk to me, including my staff.

As the timer chimes, I whoop and cheer inside my head, then just walk out of the kitchen, and into my office.

A heavy sigh breezes past my lips as my bum touches the leather seating of my chair.

My eyes close and my body just loosens, shoulders curling in.

I lift my legs, but pain lances down my calves, my muscles groaning in protest for a beat or two. My body shudders, and I moan, lips parting, my ankle smarting, but slowly they relax.

I slump in the chair, eyes going up, staring at the ceiling.

Another successful day.

Another day of keeping my mind occupied on something else other than my past.

Another day of void and hollowness.

This day hasn't been any different than the others in the past decade.

It's lonely.

Empty.

Dead.

Just what I want and will continue to keep it like this.

I don't need—

A knock on my office door stops my train of depressing thoughts, and fills me with a load of irritation.

"What?" I bark, knowing full well it's my staff.

Please don't let them call me out.

Please don't let them call me out.

I hope to gods, no one wants to meet me.

"Chef, a patron wants to meet you," Andrea, my other waitress, speaks.

I close my eyes, and count to ten.

One. Deep breath. *Two.* Deep breath. *Three...*

After I am done, I count backwards.

Counting helps me cool down. It's a technique my therapist suggested to me a few years ago.

Most days it works, but today I want to scream at someone.

My therapist recommended this technique to even my temper whenever I feel like exploding on someone.

"C-chef?"

"I am coming!" I bark again, and push my chair back, and stand.

Cursing, I walk toward the door and jerk open it. Andrea is holding a tray to her chest, trembling.

"Where?" I glare at her.

She points her shaking finger toward a table, her eyes wide as saucers. "T-table number two."

I scowl and jerk my chin, and walk briskly toward the table.

Every step is heavy and angry.

Rocks and mountains.

I'm sure people must see smoke coming out of my ears, because they literally make way for me, running away, rushing out of my path.

Me a blazing tornado.

An angry storm.

That's what happens when you disturb me assholes. This is my time.

I'm going to put a board out that says, "Chef is not available after so and so time."

Then they'll make an appointment, and I'll make sure my appointment calendar is always full.

Full like the air inside the balloon.

As I near the table, I see Rosemary, the previous mayor and one of the first few citizens—basically the owner—of this town. In fact, the town is named by her. She's sitting with the current town Mayor, Chance Knight, and another man.

I can't see his face. His back is to me.

Rosemary sees me coming, and her eyes light up.

I scowl and frown. I should have known it would be her.

She's the only one who will demand to meet at this hour, making me come out of my office.

I plant my hands on my hips and greet them. "Rosemary, Mayor."

"Finny, how are you?" Rosemary gives me one of her innocent smiles. Which she is not.

I do not buy that smile. Not for a second.

Rosemary is one of those people, you know, a mama bear to all, looks after the town. A protector. She's tough, but fair.

And most importantly, she likes to meddle… a lot.

She's a busybody who can't sit quietly, and has to always meddle. She's the town matchmaker according to me, if you ask me.

I secretly like her meddling ways, but only when it is focused on other people.

"Earth to Finny!"

The train of thoughts stop and I snap toward her. "Yeah, what?"

"You were lost in your head."

You have no idea.

"Yeah. Just work stuff." I wave a dismissive hand in the air.

"So, how have you been, Finny?"

"Finnick," I correct her. "Same as I was yesterday, Rosemary."

"Yes, yes, I can see that." She rolls her eyes, but that doesn't stop her lips from curving.

"The food was amazing," the Mayor stated.

Obviously.

People can call me arrogant, but I know my worth. I'm an excellent chef. All the certificates and awards are proof of it. "Thank you." I make a half bow. "I'm glad you guys enjoyed it." My lips flatten, and all I want to do now is get out of here.

"Finny, I want you to meet someone."

I hate that gods-damned name.

I don't know why the hell she keeps calling me that.

It grates on my nerves.

"This is Oscar Nutter. He is the owner of Plan me Up. They do event planning, you know, planning and coordinating, budgeting and scheduling, and things like that."

A soft growl vibrates at the back of the my throat. "I know what event planning is." I scowl at her, cursing silently for wasting my time.

"Okay, Mr. McGrooch. Now stop scowling and meet him."

I turn toward this Oscar man, and my knees buckle, legs are ready to give out.

I grip the back of his seat to hold myself up.

Our gazes lock. Pale green meets black

Air sticks in my lungs. Locked and sealed.

Charged air. Heated, yet cold.

Blood rushes up, roaring in my ears.

A zap of shock jolts down my spine, spreading into my veins when his lips part, and words come.

"Hello. It's nice to meet you."

The words echo between us, seeping into my skin and vibrating through my body, my soul.

Strong.

Marking.

Claiming.

Everything fades.

Every single thing around us.

A kernel of fire generates at the center of my core. Burning, spreading like a wildfire.

Tripping.

Twisting.

Treading.

I clench my hands into fists at my sides, my toes curling inside my shoes.

The twitching in my brows stops, but my heart? My heart drums, loudly, screaming inside my chest.

Mine.

Ours.

Possess.

A snort skittles out of me.

He's not mine. He isn't. Not now, not ever! And I do not, will not possess him.

Sure, the man is gorgeous, with a perfect jawline, with golden stubble, semi-full lips, a pierced eyebrow, pale green eyes, dirty-blond hair, sun-kissed skin.

Still, that doesn't mean I want to bone him.

Nope.

I like the way my life is. Happy to be alone.

Possessing someone, letting them in only for them to choose someone else later and leave me—yeah no, thank you.

Been there, done that.

Woe is me. Just about sums it up all.

"Hi." The word comes out harsher than I was intending.

Tight.

Snappish.

His—Oscar's head jerks back, shock filling in his eyes. It clears quickly, and irritation replaces it.

He bows his head in greeting and looks away, and the loss of his gaze on me is tremendous. It sends a hollow pang through my chest, leaving me somewhat breathless and aching.

"Now that you have met him. I wanted to talk to you about something. Please take a seat."

Grumbling under my breath, I wait for Oscar to make some space for me to sit.

He moves, briskly, not looking at me.

"Let's hear it then." I rest my hand on the table and look at Rosemary and Chance Knight.

"Oscar is hosting a sort of thank-you party just before Christmas at the Community center for the Vale Valley residents. His way of showing his gratitude."

How very generous of him.

She looks at me pointedly.

What? I raise my brows, questioningly. Does she expect me to be like him?

Abso-fucking-lutely not!

I bare my teeth, bristling.

I'm perfect the way I am.

She rolls her eyes and focuses her attention back on Oscar, but not before clicking her tongue at me.

Whatever.

"What's the date of the event, hon?" Rosemary inquires.

"December 21st. It's an evening event," Oscar speaks softly.

"Yeah, so we wanted to talk to you about catering the event. He wants a mix of cuisine served for the event. And I thought of you."

"Thanks for the consideration," I drawl, sarcasm dripping in every word of mine.

I'm not in the mood to be polite and considerate. They shouldn't have disturbed my Me-time.

"Yes, yes, let's get all that out of the way. You are thankful, and I'm happy to recommend you. Now, where were we? Oh, yes, so will you cater?"

If I say no, she'll badger me until I agree to victual the event.

I sigh and rub the back of my neck, then guide my fingers

into my hair, scratching my scalp, and twisting my lips. "How many are attending?" The words come out tight.

"The whole town!"

"I need numbers. Exact number of plates to be served."

"So you'll do it?" Her eyes spark, hopefulness welling in them.

"I'll do it," I grit the words out, my nails poking into my palms.

"See, I told you he'll do it." She claps, beaming.

"Are you sure?" Oscar finally looks at me, his body inclining toward me. "If you have other commitments, or are busy on that day, I can look—"

"I said I'll do it!" I snap, and regret immediately when hurt flashes in his eyes.

"Okay. Fine." He gives me a tight smile, and looks away, muttering something under his breath.

"Oh, don't mind him, Oscar. Finny here is a grooge."

"Grooge?"

"Yeah, you know, like how there's a Scrooge for a stingy man, there's a grooge for a grouchy man." Rosemary points her chin toward me, "And our beloved Finny here is the town grooge."

I love this woman.

I respect this woman.

I love this woman.

I respect this woman.

I remind myself and chant the words in my head again and again and again.

I really respect and love this woman, but she does't need to know. Only she has the balls to deal with a broken honey badger.

I narrow my eyes, and my nostrils flare when she winks at me.

"He wakes up being a grouchy soul. He's a good egg, so don't mind his words." She grins.

I grind my teeth, clenching my jaw so tight and hard they hurt.

This is the reason I need someone else to manage stuff like this, so I have minimum contact with other souls.

"I'll contact you when I have prepared a menu for the event. Leave your number at the cash register. And I'll need the list of the total number of attendees for the event at least a month before."

"Okay. Thank you. I'll do that. Shall we sign a contract?"

"There's something you should know before we shake hands on this. On the day of the event, I'll be handling the food arrangements."

"What do you mean?"

"The set up, the serving, the staff. Everything."

"But I have a—"

I raise my hand to stop him. "My people, and only my people will handle the food station. No one else. I don't trust others. My staff know what needs to be done, what I like, how I like things." I cut him a flat stare, pressing him to understand that it's my way or the highway when it comes to food stuff.

For a long charged minute, we stare at each other. His eyes condemning me without uttering a word. Cursing me to hell.

Been there, not a fun place to live at all.

"Fine," he says through his gritted teeth. "It's a deal."

Good. Good.

Then why do I feel like I have made a mistake.

CHAPTER 2

OSCAR

*A*lphahole. Highest order of grumpy, grouchy, possessive Alphahole. The worst kind. The king of Alphahole, that's what he is.

How dare he talk to us like that?

How dare he treat us like... like... like nothing.

He could have been polite, if not to me then at least to Rosemary.

She's the nicest person I know after my parents.

A little politeness and some kindness wouldn't harm his burning ass.

Arrogant Grooge.

The name suits him.

I huff silently, calling him all sorts of names inside my head. And I don't call people names. Like never.

Never. Ever.

I'm a nice guy. I don't curse, swear, or get angry. I don't huff or puff. I don't—I'm not this person. I look down at myself, hating the tension in my body, the way I'm still cursing him.

This... this wretched man has made me do all of them.

I don't like this.

Don't like the man I have been in the last thirty minutes.

The heat coming off him... it sears into me, sending a jolt of desire streak through me.

A beat later, a full body shudder ripples through me, when his elbow grazes my arm.

"Are you okay, darling?" Rosemary's concern filled voice penetrates through my internal Ted-talk.

Crap!

I force my head up and meet her gaze, my lips curving automatically. "Yeah. Just thinking about the event."

A snort, loud and clear, comes from beside me.

My head jerks in the man's direction and I cut him a glare.

What the hell is his problem?

I try to look down my nose at him, at this... this... nobody rabid cougar.

Who does he think he is to look down his nose at us like that?

A sad and bloated old horn-meister, that's who.

Not that he's old-old. But he definitely looks the part. As for being a horny-meister, that's debatable.

When was the last time he washed his face and looked in the mirror? Never, I guess.

He's going to be a bear of man to work with, I just know it.

Maybe I should ask my assistant to take care of the future meetings with Finnick.

I'm second guessing my decision to work with him. If this is how he is for a single meeting, gods help me when I have to meet him at other times to discuss the event.

He huffs and crosses his arms over his chest.

"What?" I whisper hiss, so only he can hear.

His lips flatten and eyes darken, dipping to my lips. He licks the corner of his lips, sending my heart into overdrive.

I gasp and roll my lower lip between my teeth as desire shoots down my spine, and between my legs.

What. The. Hell?

I avert my gaze, and let out the chestful of air locked inside my lungs, my heart still thundering against it.

Don't look at him.

Don't open your mouth.

His knee brushes against mine, and I inhale a sharp breath through my teeth, swallowing a moan that is eager to spill out.

How can his eyes... a mere look from him have such an effect on me?

I look down at the semi I'm sporting.

Shit!

Fuck!

Damn it!

This is not good.

This man is dangerous.

I cannot afford to sport a hard-on every time I'm in his presence. I'll be a laughing stock.

I might even get put in jail for public indecency.

I should stay far away from him. Avoid this man as much as I can.

Maybe communicate with him through calls and emails, instead of meeting him face to face.

Maybe I should ask my assistant to coordinate with him, that way I can get out of meeting and talking to him.

Maybe I should just hire someone else entirely to cater the event. But then Rosemary will have questions about all the why's and what's and all that. And honest to gods, I don't have a logical answer for her questions.

I can't just say, *"Mister Grooge ignites my fire. His grouchy self zaps my dick in attention."* Or that I'm attracted to him.

Which I'm not. Nuh-uh, I'm not.

He's not my type. I don't like grouchy, brooding Alpha-hole males. I like my men sweet and caring, and smiling.

And Finnick screams brooding, dark, dominating. All fine qualities, but it just doesn't do it for me.

No place for darkness in this sunshine's life.

I'm sure he doesn't even like flowers, or chocolates. I just know it.

"Well, now that that's settled, I'm gonna take your leave. I'll see you both at the annual Halloween Party in five days. Do not miss it."

"I'll be there," I tell her.

"I'm not sure I can make it," he murmurs.

"Nuh-uh, none of that. You are coming, that's it. You've always skirted around attending it. And last year you barely stayed for more than ten minutes."

"You know it's *not* my thing," he grits the words, his eyes hard.

Rosemary's eyes widen and she gapes. "Halloween is *everyone's* thing."

"Well, it's not mine." He snaps, and looks away.

I watch him. Study him.

He grinds his teeth, fist clenching and unclenching over his chest. He's so tense, something will break inside him if he doesn't loosen up.

What's eating him?

Something, an emotion I haven't ever felt for others, I feel for him.

Pity.

I don't pity others. There's no place for it in life. Sympathize? Yes, but never pity others.

But today I pity him.

Chance Knight opens his mouth to say something, but Rosemary cuts him off. "Finnick, you need to come."

"I'll think about it."

"No think—"

"Rosemary, leave him be. He'll come if he's in the mood." I plead to her with my eyes to leave him alone. My eyes constantly darting between the two of them.

"Okay. Fine. I'll leave it up to you. But I would definitely like it if you could come and have some fun," she says, getting up, but stops in front of him and cups his cheeks in her palms. "Open it again, Finnick. Let it in." She leans down and kisses his temple, then wordlessly walks out of the diner.

Chance Knight gets up, nods toward me, then looks Finnick in the eyes. "Listen to her." Chance pats Finnick's shoulders and follows Rosemary out.

I sit silently, wringing my hands on my lapel, unsure what to say or do.

I think it's time for me to get the hell out of here as well.

"I think I should get going as well."

He turns toward me and our gazes meet.

Hollow. His eyes are hollow. Empty.

There's so much sadness, anger, and grief in them.

Old, festering grief is wrapped around him like a blanket.

I want to wrap him in my arms, and just hug him. Hug him and hold him, and tell him everything will be alright. Bring the spark back into his eyes, revive his heart back to life, erase the sadness drowning him.

I know he will not appreciate it. I know he will push me, curse me, and still I want to do it.

I raise my hand to touch him… he flinches, leaning away. I immediately pull my hand back, my face heating up.

This is what happens when you do something you shouldn't.

And his reaction? It's a slap to my face. Hard, resounding

slap. I'm sure every patron in the diner must have heard the invisible smack.

This is so embarrassing. I shouldn't waste any more time here. I'm bound to do or say something and make a fool of myself.

"Take care," I say, and get up, and wait for him to move, or make space for me to pass.

He gets up and moves aside, his gaze downward, unable to meet my eyes.

I pass him, my hand brushing against his, and a jolt zaps through me, sending my pulse thundering.

I gasp and step away from him, then another step, putting some distance between us, but stop and turn toward him, unable to stop myself and the words wanting to come out. "I don't know what you have suffered. I don't know what you have been through in your life, but life is long and vacant and lonely when you have closed off yourself to others. Just a smidge of happiness can lessen the void inside you." I pause and take a breath. "This town is the best, and wonderful, and magical. The people of this town are wonderful. They always have your back. *Always*. I was born here. I grew up here. I have friends and family here. It's because of them that life is easy to live and experience."

"But you will lose them someday. All of them." The words are barely more than a whisper. "And the pain of losing everyone you love will be greater than anything you have ever experienced."

I nod, my lips curve into a sad smile. "Yes, I will lose them. I definitely will. But not knowing my family, nor having my friends in my life for even a day, is so much sadder than losing all of them. I'll cherish every second I get to spend with the people I love. Sure I'll be sad when they are gone, but I'll remember the happy times I got to spend with them. I will forever remember the love I got to experience because of them."

Absolute silence falls inside the diner. The fraught silence plagues me, getting on my fluttering nerves.

Finnick finally looks at me, gazing into my eyes. "Enduring all that again and again—"

"Is worth it, Finnick. So, *so* worth it." I cut him off. "All you need to do is open it again." I squeeze his arm for emphasis.

His eyes shine with some unknown emotion, but soon they set into neutrality, hiding everything from the world.

From me.

"Well, if it's worth it, then good. But I'm not going to play a fool's game. I'm happy the way I am." Finnick gives me a tight smile.

His words are hollow, as hollow as the core of a straw.

A lie.

Fear laden.

With a small kernel of hope in them.

"When you are ready." I smile and circle away, walking away from him, yet not.

I feel the weight of his gaze pressing on me, my skin tingling with awareness as I walk out of the diner.

Those four words mean more to me than him, and yet I couldn't help saying them.

Why, though?

Why does it matter if he's ready or not? If he'll open his heart or not?

Because my heart wants him to. It demands it from him.

Foolish heart. Doesn't it know that need and want are two different things?

They are woebegone curses.

CHAPTER 3

FINNICK

'**ve** done my job. I have attended the party, have shown my face, have done the meet and greet. I have even drunk the wine and some champagne, eaten a bite or two of the appetizers.

I even dressed for the occasion… Not.

I'm in my chef uniform. I have been dressed for the party since noon.

Have I been eager to attend the party? No, I have not been eager. I came here directly from the diner. Didn't have the patience to go home and change and get dressed up.

Attending the party as a chef is cool.

Now Rosemary cannot complain or pester me about never attending her Halloween party.

The mansion is lit up with lights and Halloween decorations. The whole town is attending it.

Most of the crowd are dressed in costumes, while several are in plain clothes.

People are drinking and chattering. In a nutshell, they are having fun."

I have heard whispers that one more couple in Vale Valley

is hosting a Halloween party at their place tonight, and many are planning to attend that as well, just as soon as they are done attending this one.

Good for them. I don't think I can do anymore peopling tonight.

I have seen and met enough souls, shaken enough hands to last me a lifetime.

There's only so much smiling, saying hellos, and bowing my head in greeting I can do.

I see a few people leave the party from my vantage point.

They must be heading to attend the other couple's party.

What's the couple's name? Kingsley something?

No, no. Not Kingsley.

Oh, yeah, it's Kinsley and Chester Kingston.

I have heard they live on the edge of the town. Very country-ish.

Good for them.

Wish I could get a house far away from the hustle and bustle. Life would be so much peaceful, but there were no ready to move in houses available when I was looking. And I didn't have the patience then to build a house from scratch when I was relocating to the town.

It is something I'll have to live with.

Doesn't matter now, I have a home to live in. It's a little small, but it does for me, because it comes with a big piece of land. Almost two acres, and it's on the hill a little away from all the hustle and bustle, but not isolated enough. When I decide to renovate and add more rooms, I will have the space to do so in the future.

I take a sip and continue with my people watching.

The people press and brush against me as they walk around, wishing anyone and everyone happy Halloween.

My stomach roils, as one touches my hand, eyes gleaming and glazed.

My throat closes in, and my mouth turns arid.

I curl my fingers, the nails biting into my palm. A burning sting spreads over my hand.

I push away, far back against the wall in the back, keeping a very, very healthy distance between me and everyone else.

Yet the walls keep pushing in, pressing around me.

My chest tightens, the noose around my throat being pulled painfully hard.

Leave! my brain screams. *Leave now!*

I should. This is not my scene. I don't belong here. People don't interest me. Never have.

I force air into my lungs. Long dragged breaths filling against my tense ribs and hammering heart.

It's time to go home.

Time to end this farce.

I can't bear to be here for another minute.

I take a flute of champagne from the passing waiter, my hands shaking, spilling some of the drink in my hand.

I drink it in three gulps, then place the glass on a nearby table, turn on my heel and walk toward the entrance, shaking and trembling.

I bolt, elbowing my way through the packed space, my feet pounding hard, hurried steps bringing me out of the packed mansion.

I make it without being stopped or interrupted by any of the guests. I close my eyes and stand on the steps for a long moment.

Just stand and breathe.

I shouldn't have come here. Shouldn't be here.

Why the hell have I come here tonight? Why?

So I don't disappoint Rosemary.

I love and respect her. She's the closest to a friend I have other than my brother-in-law in my life.

She's the only person in my life right now who's sticking

by me. Even though she's not family—blood family—she still acts like family.

I can never forget the sadness and shock in her eyes when I told her I didn't want to attend tonight's party.

And the devastated look behind her shock when I told her Halloween is not my thing? That was a knife in my gut.

I don't like disappointing her, but I can't help be that guy. Loss has turned me into a boorish, unrefined man. I'm never a good company.

I open my eyes and look upward into the obsidian sky, tiny bright lights glittering, shimmering, an ornament in celestial empyrean to ameliorate the vast galaxy to naked eyes. And the moon, a lonely spectacle to its magnificence, is blanketed under the curtain of coveys of clouds.

They remind me of Rohan and—

I shut out the thought and close my eyes again. My chest constricts painfully, the pain spreading into my veins.

Opening my eyes, I exhale a sigh and run my fingers through my unruly hair, still looking up into the depthless sky.

I need a haircut. It has grown too long.

And I need to get a life if looking at the sky is making me so maudlin.

"Hey!"

I still, and cautiously bring my head down, and look into the pale green eyes that have been haunting me in my nightmares the last couple of days.

The one that has been giving me wet dreams, blue balls, and palpitations.

"Hey." My voice has suddenly turned raspy.

"Are you planning to go inside?" Oscar nods behind me.

I shake my head.

Oscar inclines his head to the side, the skin around his eyes bunching slightly with curiosity.

"I did my duty of attending the party. Stayed for almost..." I look down at the watch on my hand. "...thirty minutes."

"Oh, okay. So are you, like, going back home?"

I dip my head. "Yes. But I'm thinking of just walking the street for sometime before heading home."

"That sounds nice." A soft smile curves his lips, lighting his eyes.

"Do you want to join me?" The words come out, and I want to smack myself for asking him.

I clench my teeth and push a breath out between my teeth, unable to believe what I have done.

Why the fuck am I asking him to join me? I don't need him.

He stills. "Yeah," he said. "I would like that."

Indecision wars within me, unable to decide what I should say.

Yes, or should I just tell him I changed my mind and I'm going home straight from here.

Decisions. Decisions. Decisions.

To hell with it.

"Great," I mutter. "Let's go." I take a step, but freeze when someone whoops inside the mansion. "Or do you want to go inside and attend the party? It's alright if you want to."

This time it's his face that twists with indecision, eyes constantly darting between me and the mansion. He opens his mouth to say something, but presses his lips into a thin line and looks behind me once more.

Right.

The party.

"I'll see you around," I say and walk down the steps, passing him.

I still, his fingers coiling around my arm, his breath kisses my warm skin, and his words zap a rush through my veins. "Let's go," he whispers.

One corner of my lips tug up, and something loosens inside me.

I nod and walk, his fingers still wrapped around my arm, and I don't lose the half smile I'm sporting.

We walk the streets in silence, enjoying the cool night breeze caressing us, crickets chirruping, singing, trees dancing to the drifting wind's tune. The whole thing reminds me of—

I block the thought, shoving it to the back of my mind, in a box, where it needs to be.

Those dark memories have no place in my life right now.

I watch as kids and adults walk the streets in their costumes dressed for Halloween, trick or treating from house to house, collecting candies.

Where I come from, we don't celebrate this Halloween, but we do harvest the fall crops and pray to the God, Kala Bhairava, to keep them from evil souls who want to corrupt and destroy them.

Sometimes I wonder why I've traveled all the way here, crossing the ocean, flying over the mountains to come to Vale Valley all those years ago.

I haven't left this town once I came here, not even to take a vacation.

This magical town has given me peace when I badly needed it.

I didn't sleep for days when I first arrived here. As soon as I found a place to rent I slept for a whole week.

Didn't wake to use the restroom, or even to drink water.

I just slept.

Dead to the world.

In a way, I was then.

I'm still dead, I think.

"Do you want to play a fun game?"

I stumble over myself, my steps faltering.

"What?" I blink, and blink a few times more, wanting to clear the web of torment from my head.

"Let's play a game." His lips pull back, showing his white teeth.

I stop us in the middle of the road and face him. "Oookay."

With a wary amusement, he leans into me, squeezing his fingers, and jerks his chin. "No need to stop. We can walk and still play this game. You'll love it, I promise."

"Alright." We resume walking, and Oscar explains how the game is played. It's called hashtag your sex life. The most hilarious answer will win a dinner treat.

"Okay, I'll go first. Hashtag I don't have time. Now your turn. Tell me about your sex life with a hashtag."

Am I really doing this? Play this silly game with him?

I swallow hard. Hard enough that I'm sure it is audible in the next few towns.

"Come on, play the game. You know you want to. I can see the curiosity in your eyes. Go on tell me."

Oh, fuck it. Looks like I'm going to play this game.

Alright then.

I lick my lips, and look around us to make sure no one is close by to hear me, my nerves fluttering and tingling. "Okay." I nod and fill my lungs with air. "Hashtag at least it vibrates."

Oscar chokes on his laugh, his eyes going large. "W-what!" He sputters.

"You asked for it." I shrug my shoulders, my face heating, looking like a ripe tomato. I give him a side eye, but still keep an eye on our surroundings. "If you don't like my answer, then maybe we should stop."

"No, no, no. Nothing like that. You just surprised me. I'm just... marveling at your answer."

"Sure you are." I roll my eyes.

"I am." He clears his throat. "My turn. Hashtag infrequent due to exhaustion."

Really? I don't believe him. And I show him my disbelief in my eyes.

"What? It's true. I'm too exhausted after working all day to bother doing anything else. The only thing on my mind after a long day is sleep. Anyway, it's your turn."

"Okay. Hashtag nobody does me better than me."

He hollers, his body shaking. A few passersby give us curious stares, some muttering under their breath, calling us eccentric.

Oscar bends down at the waist, holding his sides, panting, but still laughing. He takes a few deep breaths then straightens, and looks me in the eyes. His eyes shimmering with happiness. "My gods, you are bloody good at this game, man. I'll have to take some pointers from you."

"I'm just stating the facts of my life," I mutter under my breath, words barely a whisper.

"What? Did you say something?"

"I said, it's your turn now. Go on, say it."

"Okay. Let me think for a moment." He scratches his chin for a beat, and then suddenly his face brightens. "Oh, oh, I have one. Hashtag can we clear out the cobwebs today."

Seriously? My eyes wander down toward his crotch, tucked behind his pants. He's dressed as a paramedic, and he looks good in them.

Oscar smacks me on the arm, his eyes darkening, blazing. "Get your eyes off my junk," he says haughtily, though his words belie the desire simmering in his eyes.

"Alright, alright. You can't blame a man for wondering how dense your cobwebs are."

He growls, flushing.

It's cute.

I freeze and my breath hitches.

Cute? Since when have I started noticing someone's growl is cute?

Since meeting Oscar.

Fuck.

Fuck, fuck, fuck.

Okay, brain stop with this cheesy stuff. Play the game, then shut up.

"Your turn."

Right.

"Hashtag never better, just add batteries."

"Ohh, that's a good one." He chuckles. "Okay, so hashtag at least the pinky vibrates."

I choke on my breath and start coughing, my eyes watering from the surprise.

His hands find their way over to my back and rub gently, awakening a storm inside me.

Getdowngetdowngetdown, I scream in my head, eyes lowered at my crotch.

Don't you fucking stand up.

"Are you alright?"

"Fine. Just fine," I rasp, and straighten, averting my gaze, avoiding his eyes.

I look at our surroundings and realize we have arrived near the woods. "I think we should head back. It's dark and I need to get up early tomorrow."

"Do we have to," Oscar groans, his face scrunching. "It's such a beautiful night. Twinkling sky, stars and moon playing hide and seek behind the clouds, cool breeze, just magnificent. Soon, we won't have nights like this for the next few months."

"So what do you want to do?"

"Let's just enjoy it. We can walk in the woods, just take a stroll around there."

"Are you sure it's a good idea? It's dark and gods know what things are dwelling inside the dark forest."

"This is Vale Valley, Finnick. It's a sweet, magical town. Nothing bad dwells in here. We are safe."

I know that. I really really do. I trust this town, its people. This town is magical, it protects its habitants.

It's not the others I'm worried about, I'm worried about me. Staying with Oscar deep within the forest, away from the crowd, in such close proximity with no one to chaperone us… I may do something I'll regret for the rest of my life.

He'll think I've lured him here to take advantage of him. He'll mark me as a predator, which I'm not. I'm a honey badger, we don't hunt. We are the hunted.

"Come on, let's go. We are shifters, and we can see clearly in the dark without having to use our cellphone flashlights." He pulls my hand, dragging me into the forest.

I sigh and give in. "Alright, alright. Let's go."

I give my brain a ted talk to not act like a rutting Alpha.

Which I am.

I tell my brain to have some control over the lust brewing inside me.

Which it is.

I tell my brain to get inline with my heart and listen to it.

Which it never does.

The story of my life.

As we enter the forest, venturing deeper into it, we are surrounded by giant and strong trees. The forest smells of morning and pine, and the trees of heaven.

I breathe in the fresh air and walk with him, silence and insects as our only companions. The branches sway whenever a gust of wind rushes past, sending goosebumps across my body.

We are almost at the center of the forest when several owls call out, hooting loud enough to tear my eardrums off.

Hootiedoom! My brain screams and I shiver, dread curling in the pit of my stomach.

I look around us, head swiveling in every direction I can manage, fearing I may have missed something, an intruder maybe.

Sweat beads on my forehead, and neck, and back, running down my spine.

Oscar squeezes my hand, and I look him in the eyes. His eyes are a little glassy, and a lot darker than before.

"Finnickkk," he purrs, one side corner of his lips curving up. He sways slightly, his breathing a little shallower than before.

I adjust my body and face him, gripping his shoulders in my hands. "Are you okay, Oscar?"

"I'm fantastic, Finnick. Just marvelous." His mouth curves into a big smile.

"Maybe I should take you home."

"Oh, live a little," he drawls, and loops his arms around my neck, his words slurring. He leans forward and sniffs my scent, his tongue darting out and licking a strip of flesh on my neck.

I freeze and my breath hitches.

"You taste so good. So salty and minty, and just you," he croons.

My mouth drops open and my eyes become wide saucers. He's just licked me. Just rolled his tongue out and slurped my sweat.

Hot damn!

Erotic.

Sweat beads on his face as well.

It's a cool, pleasant night. Then, why the hell are we sweating so much?

Oscar presses himself to me, rubbing his body.

Oh, shit!

Fucking fuck!

A drop of his sweat lands on the side of my neck, and I suppress the moan wanting to escape. I want to stop myself, but I can't and sniff his scent.

Pine and spring.

The scent of his arousal and sweat has every Alpha instinct rising inside me with a heady speed.

I take a deep breath, and try to untangle myself from him. However, he just tightens his arms more, his tongue flicking, dancing across my heated flesh.

I curse and swear under my breath when he grinds his pelvis against me. "You smell so good," he sniffs. "So, so good."

"Thanks, I guess."

My cock hardens when his lips move up, and his hands slide down my spine to my ass.

"Fuck." The curse comes out before I can rein it in.

"I want you, Finnick. I want you so much," he says, brushing his lips against mine.

A tremor shudders through me, my fingers coiling harder on his shoulder, pulling a moan out of him.

My breathing turns ragged, my heart thunders violently inside my chest as his fingers knead my ass, his warm breath skimming over my lips.

The mounting urge to bone him is getting stronger and stronger and stronger.

The urge to own him, bedevil him, dominate him are the only thoughts ringing in my head.

Claim him, my head screams.

Mark him, my heart pleads.

Worship and ravage him, my soul demands.

Ours! They all sing together.

I feel lightheaded as he bites my clammy skin. A growl rips out of my mouth, and my fingers bite into him.

"Please, Finnick, I want you. Take me!" he screams, panting, shivering, his hands skating over to my front, stroking,

A moment, a lifetime, an eternity. I look into his eyes. Just look into them.

Even though they are hazy and lost, the words are true in every emotion that is skimming through them.

Everything in me narrows to one emotion swimming in them the strongest.

Desire for me.

Me.

The moon illuminates its light upon us, casting the glow like a spotlight, an essence, influencing my desire for him, and his for me, sparking my lust, growing my need.

With a growl, I crash my lips against his, needing to taste him. It starts slow, light and sensual, but turns savage when he bucks his hips, pressing his pelvis into me.

Something snaps inside me as the zing of our connection spreads through my blood, rushing down south, then I'm all over him.

My lips pulling him, my hands gripping him, teeth looking for a soft spot to sink into.

"More," he growls, his hips rotating, pulse rushing. "Please, more."

The words break the thin control I have, bringing out the Alpha inside me.

Instinct overcomes me, making me lift him, holding him against me.

Oscar immediately snakes his legs around my hips, his fingers making their way into my hair, gripping, holding on for dear life.

He pulls, and pulls, and pulls on my hair, the pain barely a nick in the grand scheme of things nature has for us. For it is nature that is making me do these things.

I, in no way, am capable of climbing him, rutting like a horny dog.
But that is what I am doing right now.
A rutting Alpha.
A rutting honey badger.
An Alpha in heat.
Fuck my life!
But who cares. All I want to do is own him.
And I will.

Finnick

CHAPTER 4

FINNICK

I'm not me, yet I am.

The body is mine, yet it is not.

His arousal rubs against me, sending friction after friction of pleasure to my groin.

"Need you."

The word roil through me like an intonate, vibrating, besmearing like a salve to revive me.

My soul.

I put him down, our lips locked again, and rip his clothes off with a growl. Off comes his shirt and his pants.

"Off!" He pants, glazed eyes frantically looking at my clothes. Hands push my torque blanche off my head, rake my apron, tearing open my double-breasted jacket, and shove my pants down.

The heat coming off him seeps into my flesh, his scent filling my nostrils, blazing my lust.

I push him against a tree, grab the back of his head and pull him closer and lower his lips to mine.

I nip his bottom lip, grazing my teeth over the stinging flesh.

My mouth roves down his neck, kissing, nipping, licking.

He pulls out of my hold, then falls on his knees in front of me before I can halt him, and wraps his mouth around my aching dick, his hands diving behind me, groping my ass.

I growl as he feasts on me, my tether on my sanity dwindling with every stroke of his tongue.

I moan as he takes in my full length, his teeth grazing my sensitive flesh, sending a zing down my spine to my balls.

"Fuck."

His tongue makes contact with my too-full balls, and I hiss, throwing my head back.

My fingers find their way to his hair, holding his head in place, and thrust inside him, hitting the back of his throat.

Not once does he gag or make retching noises.

My pace increases, pleasure builds, tingling at the base of my spine, sending a buzz through my veins.

My cum ready to explode.

However, I don't want to come in his mouth.

I want to fill his ass.

I unclench my fingers and pull out of his mouth, drawing a whine out of him.

I hook my fingers under his arms and lift him, then kiss him with fevered urgency, rubbing my shaft against his.

"My turn," I say, and trail open-mouthed kisses across his neck, down his chest. "I'm going to do such filthy things to you, you'll see stars." My tongue flicks his nipple. "Bright, colorful stars, that'll leave you breathless."

"Yes, p-please," he stutters, then moans as my tongue flicks over his peaked nipple. I kiss it, suck it, roll it between my teeth, then bite it.

Every movement heaving a moan, a groan and several whimpers from him.

Each sound echoes through the cool night, the trees and insects and wind our only witnesses.

To our depravity.

To libertinage.

Unforgettable vice.

I give attention to his other nipple, bringing him to the periphery of sin.

"So sweet, so responsive. Made just for me." The words flow, plenty of truth and some disbelief.

My lips move, again trailing down open-mouthed kisses down to his abdomen.

I go down, down, down, until his erect dick is in front of me, brushing my chin.

I lick the crown, tasting his precum.

"Do you think your cum will taste as sweet and as savory as your precum?" He mumbles something unintelligible. "Don't know? Let's find out then."

I look up and repeat it again, evoking a hiss out of Oscar, his fingers clenching and unclenching at his side.

Keeping my eyes on him, I take half of his shaft into my mouth, licking, scraping, sucking.

He moans, his body trembling, hips rocking.

His reaction pulls a smile on my lips, my fingers sliding, gliding over his hips. I run them down to his ass, and find it soaked with his slick.

Like an omega in heat.

I don't even know if he's an omega, or something else.

From his aroused scent, he smells like an omega, but he's definitely not in heat.

Or maybe he is.

This is all the moon's doing.

The full moon tends to send shifters over the edge.

At least I think it does.

My urges are strong on a full-moon night. And I have heard that omegas ovulate strongly on a full-moon night.

I usually lock myself inside my house, but today I am out.

In the open.

Glutting a body, rutting with my mouth, my hands, and soon with my cock.

A hiss, a deep moan vibrates at the back of my throat at the prospect.

"I want to come, I need to come," Oscar cries, panting, shaking.

"You will." *In due time.*

Right now, I'm enjoying edging him.

I scrap my teeth—a bit harder than necessary—over his crown. His hips buck, and a curse spills out of his mouth. *"Fuck!"*

I savor his frustration, his insistence on coming. Begging, pleading like a good submissive.

The forest smells like sex, need, and debauchery.

Promiscuity.

Oscar's pheromones float into the air, charging the fire inside me.

My head bobs, dragging my tongue to the base of his length, licking his balls.

"P-please," he sobs, his plea reverberating through the forest.

Increasing my effort, I suck him harder and harder, and faster, bringing him to the edge and then stopping.

"Noooo, please." His body shudders, shaking violently, eyes wild and dark.

His eagerness, his helplessness awakens the Neanderthal inside me, bringing out the savage dominant.

I resume sucking him, no intention of stopping this time. I rub my fingers over the crease of his channel, spreading the slick.

I shudder when his fingers find their way to my hair and he fists it, pulling harder and painfully with every stroke of my tongue over his cock.

I'm peaked too, ready to shoot my load, but I want to do it inside him.

Fill his ass with my cum, keep it locked there. But, before that, I want to fill his ass with his own cum.

The image sends a dizzy spell through my head, my body trembling with carnal desiderating.

Certain and constant as the diurnal tides.

Ceaseless.

Deathless.

The fire burns and burns and burns, pushing me to bring him over the fringes of pleasure.

"Come, Oscar." The words purr in the air, shimmering his release.

He tips his head back and screams my name in pleasure as he unloads his nectar into my mouth.

Again, and again, and again.

His body shudders, eyes roll back, and I can hear the thundering of his heart as he finds his high.

The whole forest can.

When I'm certain there is nothing more to erupt from his throbbing, twitching dick, I pull back, his cock sliding out of my mouth.

I grab his hips and twist his body—not giving him a chance to protest—bringing his ass into my vision.

His soft, yet firm and full ass on display in front of me breaks everything and nothing inside me.

How long has it been since I have wanted to fuck someone?

Nearly a decade, yet it feels like an eternity has passed.

I'm momentarily stunned by the admission and the realization that I will be breaking this long drought.

A promise I'd made myself when I lost everything I held dear.

Own him. He belongs to you, my heart reminds me.

A ridiculous thought and wish to have.

He never has, and will never belong to me. However, that thought doesn't stop my body from wanting him.

My brain shuts down, stopping the train of thoughts and focuses on his dripping ass.

I spread his ass, putting his slick drenched entrance on display.

Using my index fingers, I pull apart his hole, and kiss it.

Featherlight.

A phantom touch.

He moans, a shudder rippling through his being. "Oh, gods," he cries.

I quickly thrust my tongue inside his ass and tease him, stretching his opening.

Viciously.

Mercilessly.

Filling him with his own juice, slowly, sensually.

"Please... Oh, gods." He pushes his ass into my face, his body writhing, trembling violently.

"Inside me. Gods, inside me."

The words short-circuit common sense, erasing any thread of sanity, wiping away my control.

I growl, and push him toward the tree's trunk and spread his cheeks, transferring the remaining come of his from my mouth into his ass, and press my thumb over his entrance to hold it inside him.

"Stand still," I order and stand up, my knees wobbling, legs shaking, body trembling, breath coming out in short puffs.

With my free hand, I swipe some of his slick coating around his ass and spread it over my cock.

Without warning, I shove into him, driving deep, deep, deep inside him.

"Gods, yesss!" Oscar screams, his head inclined to the side. "More. Please, more!"

And more he gets. More I give.

I pull out all the way and slam back inside him, finding that sweet spot inside his ass.

I repeat the process, plugging again, and again, and again, hitting that sensitive area.

"Scream, boy. Because you are at my mercy tonight," I breathe into his ear.

"Yes!" He pounds his fists into the tree.

"Feel it," I say, my fingers finding his peaked nipples. I rub them, dragging a whimper from him. "Feel what I'm doing to you."

He sobs, his whole being shaking, shivering with need.

Mine! The animal inside me snarls.

Mine! Mine! Mine!

"Mine," I mimic the snarl, unable to stop the words from spilling out.

And not an ounce of regret fills me.

Not one iota.

My heart rejoices at the declaration, my chest expands.

And I marvel at the confused feeling mixed with elation filling me.

"Please." His plea pulls me back to him, my focus latching on bringing us both pleasure.

We are going to soar.

High and mighty.

To the stars and lights.

CHAPTER 5

OSCAR

*S*torm. The right word to describe what I'm feeling inside.

My heart jumps and stumbles and jumps again, my brain not realizing the meaning, the purpose behind his word.

I'm lost, drowning into the pool of dark pleasure.

Lightless tunnel of titillating desire.

My eyes roll back into my head as he plunges inside me, filling me to the hilt, over and over and over again.

With every plunge, with every hit to the spot, the ache between my legs intensifies, my nerves ratchet.

A shiver rushes through me, his teeth nipping and taunting, hands torturing me.

My release flames, building and building and building, coming up higher and higher, and ever higher.

Spreading in every cell of my body, fusing into my blood.

Waves after waves after waves of goosebumps cover my skin.

Finnick licks the side of my throat, his scent filling my blood.

"You want me?" He breathes.

Hell yes, I want him. I want him more than I should. More than my next breath.

"Answer me!" He nips the side of my jaw.

"Y-yes," I whimper.

He presses a kiss to the underside of my jaw, his lips trailing, leaving wet kisses all over my shoulder.

"Good." He grinds his hip, tearing me inside out obdurately.

And I love it. Love everything he's doing to me.

Love everything I'm feeling, inside and out.

I crave it.

Ache for it.

Hunger for any scraps he'll throw at me.

When have I become such a pitiful omega?

When have I let myself be used like a toy?

Never.

But tonight I'm a honey squirrel shifter, wanting an Alpha to annihilate me inside out.

If he asks me to lick his dick after peeing, I don't think I'll be able to say no, deny him anything.

I'm acting like a pathetic omega in heat, which I'm not.

I'm not in heat.

But something has happened between the walk from the outskirts to the forest.

I have been filled with lust and need to be mounted.

Savagely.

Raw.

No barrier holds.

And now the desire to be claimed, to be owned has increased ten fold.

What is happening to me?

Why is it happening to me?

I whimper, his hips moving faster and harder.

Oh, gods, I'm going to come.

I'm so close.

I close my eyes, my breath coming out fleetingly and hot.

I feel lightheaded, charged, and reckless. Finnick nips and bites the flesh over my shoulder, heightening my senses.

I'm at the edge. He's brought me there.

Him.

Mine! my soul shouts.

So loud, I think the whole town must have heard it. Or maybe it's just me, thinking, dreaming of an incandescent sky.

I turn my face and capture his lips, tongue swirling, snaking around his greedy ones, wanting to taste him.

He nips my tongue, then sucks it for good measure.

I hiss when his teeth pinch into my tongue once more, my fingers burying themselves into his sweat drenched hair.

I'm ready to dive.

I'm ready to jump off the cliff.

Ready to reach the highs I know only Finnick can bring me to.

His masterly fingers coil around my length, and pump it with great urgency, his hips thrusting unevenly.

"Give me what I want, Oscar. Scream it for me," he growls, an animal in human flesh. "Let the world know who you fucking belong to."

I know he doesn't mean them. That the words are spoken in the heat of the moment, but that doesn't stop my heart from soaring.

It doesn't stop me from hoping.

Doesn't stop me from dreaming.

"Let go, Oscar," he grunts and drives into me with such force, my eyes roll into my head, and a scream tears out of my mouth, his name on repeat on my tongue as I explode, spurt after spurt after spurt shooting out, ropes of come encrusting the tree.

His hips move erratically, and three thrusts later, he's filling my ass with his juice, his seed cramming deep into my core.

I clench around him, my hands fisting his hair, drawing several curses past his lips.

Uncoiling my fingers, I lean forward and plant my arm on the tree, then rest my forehead over it, all the while trying to fill my lungs with air.

A moment later, his shaft twitches inside my ass, then the crown of his cock...

Oh, shit!

Fuck!

Fuck, fuck, fuck.

I whimper and make a mewling noise at the back of my throat, his knot is expanding, pushing, stretching the muscles inside my ass.

Agonizingly.

At full mast.

I thrash my head from side to side, the burning inside me sharpening, making my knees buckle, and my heart to wail behind my lungs.

Starlight—sublime yet powerful, terrific yet terrifying—shimmering behind my eyes as we are locked, a strange feeling—magic—pulsing through my veins, mingles with my blood, and makes my heart stutter and stumble.

Everything ceases to exist.

The world.

My pleasure.

My being.

Except for the pain, mounting by leaps and bounds.

I explode again, my jizz squirting out of the slits on the crown of my shaft.

Fuck knows where the hell the juice again fills my dick miraculously. Where it has come from has left me drained.

It has altered something inside me. Something very small, and still not noticeable.

I moan at the change. Unable to point to it, hold it, or even accept it.

A new, far-out feeling.

Renewing.

Reborn.

It's a heady feeling. One that makes me lose consciousness.

And I embrace the darkness, letting it pull me into oblivion, forgetting the regret that I am sure will fill my being later.

WE ARE LYING down on our sides.

How we have managed to do that, I freaking have no idea. None at all.

Finnick is asleep. Thank gods, for small miracles.

I don't think I can face him after the way I have shinnied up him, groped him, ground against him like a C grade hussy.

My cheeks heat up, at a loss due to my reckless behavior, my impuissant actions.

Who was that man?

Horny teenager, that's who.

And now that the post haze has come down, my brain won't shut up thinking about tonight's fuckups.

Because everything tonight has been a huge, massive, gigantic fuckup—I might as well use the word... after all the fucked up things I have done tonight.

I don't know what has gotten into me. This is so not me. Nuh-uh.

This night will forever be etched into my mind.

I have been a different guy.

I have been a possessed man.

And I'm a guy who doesn't believe in one-night stands.

I'm a guy who believes in intimacy.

I'm a guy who believes in courting.

I'm a guy who doesn't climb another man like a tree. Unless... unless I have seen a spider.

A shudder barrels through me at the thought of seeing a spider.

I hate those eight-legged creatures.

One had bitten me when I'd visited Australia years ago. I had to be admitted to a hospital there.

It's a nightmare I always carry with me.

My body stills, heart stumbles, and tension coils into every cell of my being as Finnick mumbles something in his sleep, his hand falling off my belly, and his dick—which has been hard all this time inside me—finally slips out.

Thankyouthankyouthankyou.

I send a small prayer that he doesn't wake up. That he stays asleep. At least till I can get out of here.

Cautiously, I stand up and look for my clothes.

My shifter eyes find them immediately and I grab them, pulling on the pants first and buttoning them.

I'm grateful it's still dark, which means everyone will be asleep still, and no one will see me walking back home at this ungodly hour with my clothes askew and looking cock-eyed.

I pull on my shirt next, but stop.

Fuck. All the buttons have been ripped off. I can't button the shirt.

You ripped more than a few buttons tonight!

The reminder from my brain makes me blush like a schoolgirl.

Yeah I have done more than rip the buttons. I got my ass ripped tonight.

Which is a first for me, and last.

I'm not doing anything like this ever again. Never.

But you loved it. You loved it too much. My heart sing songs.

That doesn't mean I should repeat the mistake, because this whole thing has been a mistake.

Finnick is not my type. I have said it before, and I'll say it again. He is *not* my type.

He's growly, grouchy, and grumbly. Totally and inflexibly rough around the edges, rude, brutish, brooding.

A neanderthal.

A caveman!

I can go on. The whole dictionary and thesaurus is not enough to describe his personality.

You liked his hands across your body, inside you.

Nope, not my type.

You loved the way he kissed you, the way his tongue skimmed across your heated skin.

Still not my type.

You crave him, his touch, his scent, his everything!

Definitely not my type.

You saw a new side of him tonight. The sweet, funny, caring side.

Aah, fuck! He is my type!

I close my eyes and shake my head. Nothing good will come from this relationship if I pursue it. Nothing at all.

We are not compatible.

And if by some miracle we are, I know he will break my heart. I just know it. There is something dark about him. It's in his eyes.

The emotions swim in them.

My fingers twitch, wanting to touch him, skim my fingers through his hair, kiss those pouting lips.

Do it!

No. I shake my head, clearing the thoughts, wiping it off my brain. No, I should not.

I can't.

I won't.

I need to get out of here. I have to put an opulent amount of distance between us. Between the things we have done.

I quickly tie my shirt and put on my shoes, and walk away from him, but stop a short distance away.

I look over my shoulder, inclining my body to get a good look at him, and imprint every detail of his form. The way he sleeps, the peacefulness on his face, the way his lips move and pucker like an infant, his unruly hair, one hand tucked between his ear and shoulder, his legs crossed at the ankle.

I'll remember this and cherish it.

However, we are not meant to be together.

This is as long as my journey is with him.

You still have to work with him. You have a party to plan.

I'll cross that bridge later, but right now, I need to get out of here.

I start walking, my shifter eyes and senses guiding me out of the forest.

You are making a mistake. You'll regret it later.

I'm already regretting it. There's a heaviness in my chest, an ache so intense… if I give in it'll crumple me.

Irrevocably.

Unequivocally.

Emphatically.

However, I need some space to think, and not get distracted by his eyes, lips, and scent.

With every step that I take, with every step that I separate us, setting us apart, something shatters inside me.

Your heart.

Yeah, my heart.

What's one more ache on top of several others I'm feeling.

As I near the woodland edge, one thought comes out jarring at the forefront of my mind.

We didn't use protection.

My breath hitches, and my heart sinks into the pit of my stomach.

I'm truly fucked.

'm ashamed of myself is the understatement of the century.

Shame and guilt has been heavy on my heart, which has made me a bear of man to be around.

My kitchen staff have been more wary of me than they were before.

More scared of my wrath than they had been before.

Plus, I have been avoiding meeting or even seeing Rosemary, or anyone from her family.

And not to forget, Oscar. I have evaded Oscar like hell the last couple of weeks.

I don't take his calls.

I don't answer his emails.

I send him away when he comes to the diner, or hide in my office when he doesn't leave soon enough for my liking.

It's been a cycle of hide and seek.

I hide and Oscar seeks me.

I don't want to. I really, really don't want to hide, but the remorse that has been filling inside me has darkened my soul, piece by piece chipping my sanity with every passing second.

Coward.

Yeah, I am. I heartily agree with my head.

I'm a coward for hiding and not facing him head-on, the way I should have done the next day after our secret tryst.

When did I turn into a spineless recreant?

If my family were here right now, they would have laughed at me and would have called me a candy-ass bitch for avoiding Oscar like a weakling mouse.

You are scared!

I'm scared of nothing. Nothing.

More like contrite and pertinent of my actions and behavior.

I hope, when I'm ready and have the guts to face Oscar, he will forgive me.

I really, really hope he does.

But you miss him!

I really, really do. So much, which is crazy. I mean I have met him only twice and I'm already bonded to him in some strange way that it's hard to explain.

Hard to put into words my attraction toward him.

A knock on my office door has me straightening in my chair, my senses on high alert. No one should be here at this time.

It is past midnight.

Someone must have forgotten something. It has to be Duncan. That man is so forgetful, he is always leaving something behind. A dog has a better chance of remembering.

Mayday, mayday, my brain screams.

Another knock, and I clear my throat and answer, "Come in."

The door slowly opens, my eyes rivet to the silhouette that glides in, a shadow of a mass, and in walks Oscar.

Abort mission, abort mission.

Too late to do that.

He stands in the doorway, his lips press in a thin line.

My heart jolts, the hollow place in my heart filling with relief and dread.

I meet his gaze, his eyes blazing with rage, devil's wrath erupting in them.

I stand up, my hands fisting at my sides, the small metal binder clips biting into my palm.

"Oscar." His name, a chant and a plea on my tongue.

His nostrils flare, and those pale green orbs turn dark.

He opens his mouth, which I'm sure is to curse and inveigh me. Which I deserve.

Every name, every expression, every locution coming out of his mouth… I have earned them. I'm entitled to them.

I'll accept anything he has to say, any punishment he will hand me, but not before I say my piece.

"How are you, Oscar?" The vocable, a hoarse request.

I wince, and bite the inside of my cheek, my gaze lowering slightly.

What the fuck is wrong with me?

That's not what I have been wanting to say. Those are not the words I have been dreaming of presenting to him.

Why the hell am I asking how he is? I know how he is.

He's livid.

He's disappointed.

He's distraught.

He's incensed.

He's too many thing to fucking count.

And it is all because of me.

"How am I?" he screams. "How the fuck do you think I am when you refuse to talk to me?"

Uh, pissed. Definitely pissed.

"For weeks you have avoided me. You don't take my calls,

refuse to reply to my emails. You have the fucking nerve to send your freaking staff to tell me you are busy or not in? What. The. Actual. Fuck, Finnick? What the actual fuck?" He takes a shuddering breath, his eyes blazing, ready to tear me limb from limb. "I don't swear, but you have made me do that. I don't get angry, but I'm snapping at everyone I come face to face with. I always smile, but these days I'm just a grumpy nutter. You have destroyed me."

I round the table and stand in front of him. Cautiously, I lift my hand to touch him. "I'm sorry—"

He steps away, and shakes his head angrily. "I don't want your empty apology, Finnick. I want a fucking explanation why you have been avoiding me... Why?"

Reprobation takes every space available in my body. I cast down my eyes, unable to meet his gaze.

"Please, just tell me. Tell me why you have been avoiding me?" He pleads, his voice trembling, shoulders curling in. "Did I do something wrong? Do I disgust you? Am I not good enough for your company?" His eyes fill, voice breaking. "Tell me."

"It's not that."

"Then what is it?"

I open my mouth to explain to him, but wonder how I can best explain to him. My actions have been despicable, and there's no skirting around it.

I look down at my hands, chest heavy with regret.

I own my mistakes from that night. I hundred percent own them. I just don't know how to erase that misjudgment.

Because I really want to wipe out that night's mistake, for it *was* a mistake.

I should have had more control over my emotions, shouldn't have given in that easily. And because I didn't stop when I should have, I have ruined everything.

"It is because I molested you?"

My head snaps up, and eyes widen.

What did he just say? Did he say he molested?

"What?" I blink, my breath freezing in my lungs. I blink again, unable to believe he just said that.

"You didn't—"

"But I did! I molested you. I'm a rapist," he says frantically, his shoulders lifting and bunching tight with tension. "I'm the vilest man in Vale Valley. I should call the town sheriff and surrender myself. I don't know what came over me that night, what I was thinking suggesting we go to the forest. The forest is the last place I should be visiting on a full-moon night. And foolish of me, I invited you to go with me. This is what happens when you listen to your heart, rather than your brain—"

He gasps as I grab his shoulder, coiling my fingers to hold him in place and not let him step away from me, and stop his rambling.

"Take a deep breath." Eyes wide, he inhales a long breath and fill his lungs. "Now exhale."

As he exhales, his eyes close instinctively, shoulders coming down.

"Do it one more time." When I know he's relaxed, I guide him to the love seat in my office, then push him to sit. "Now, let's make a few things clear before you get your boxers in a bunch." I crouch in front of him and take his hands in mine, and look him in the eyes. "You didn't molest me. You didn't rape me. And you are not a vile person, so we don't need to call the town sheriff."

He opens his mouth to argue, but I shake my head to stop him.

"I was a willing party that day, Oscar. I was eager to roll in the hay when you invited me. The blame doesn't fall just on your shoulders. It shouldn't. I could have, at any time, stopped us from going any further, but I didn't."

"But I was the one who jumped on you!"

"And I let you jump on me. Like I said, I could have stopped you, but I didn't."

"Why didn't you?"

"Because I couldn't."

"But why, Finnick?"

"I just couldn't. I have wanted you too much since the day we met, but I also know there's no future for us. I cannot give you what you want, and you deserve so much more than I'm capable of giving you."

"Why can't you?"

Indecision wars within me, my heart wanting to burst out and tell him everything. But a small part of me wants to cling to my past and keep it to myself. My burden to bear. My sorrow to suffer in.

When I continue to stay silent, he leans forward and asks me softly, "Why can't you, Finnick?"

The softness in his voice and eyes undoes me, breaking my hold on the past, entangling the tether of dolor. The words tumble out.

Unstoppable.

Carelessly.

Everything spills out. Everything my heart wants him to know. "Because I'm not capable of loving again. And because my heart is not whole enough to have love in it again."

"Again?"

I nod. "I have had my epic fairytale, my one true love. I had a mate and a child, and family and friends. My life was happy and full of peace, but then everything beautiful in my life was snatched away in the blink of an eye."

"How?" He squeezes my hands for emphasis, and I look at our laced fingers.

"A pack of hungry feral hyaenas killed my entire cete. Sslaughtered them all like they were waste paper. Like their l-lives m-meant n-nothing."

My lips quiver as the image of my mate and babies lying in puddles of blood greet me.

I squeeze my eyes shut and stop the image from turning into a horror movie. My teeth sink into my lower lips, and the backs of my eyes sting.

Will I ever forget the past?

Can I ever move on from the loss?

No, never. I can never move on. I can never forget what happened to my family.

"Not many survived. A handful of people made it, but barely. I was one among them, and my brother-in-law."

A body—his body—slams into me, knocking the wind out of me, and I lose my balance. Before I fall onto my ass, I wrap my arm around him and press the heel of my other hand on the floor, and lever our bodies down.

"I'm so sorry, Finnick. So sorry for your loss," he whispers into my ears.

"Thank you," I croak.

We stay like that for several minutes, and the pressure on my wrist intensifies, somewhat numbing my arm.

Without releasing him, I slowly sit on the floor and adjust us.

I should push him, let the air come between us, but the press of his body against mine, and the heat coming off him seeps into every fiber inside me. It feels good, too good if you ask me. And that's the problem. The crux of all my thoughts always comes back to him.

I shouldn't want him, but I do.

I shouldn't be attracted to him, but I am.

My heart shouldn't breathe life into my being, but it is.

I don't know what to do. How to banish these emotions and feelings I'm having for him.

Maybe it's just my libido speaking. After not having any action for years, this is what happens when attention is thrown toward me.

I should let him go, unwrap my arms, but my heart thrashes against the bones caging around it. It detests the idea.

Too bad, buddy.

My sanity is more important than what my heart desires.

I slowly unwind my arm and grab his shoulders and push him away.

I look into his eyes, and see there are so many emotions flashing in them.

"Thank you for telling me," Oscar whispers.

I nod and lower my head and look down.

"But I'm still sorry for what I did."

My head snaps up, and I narrow my gaze.

"Before you get all angry and aggravated, let me tell you why."

I incline my head for him to go on.

"Squirrels are hyper on full-moon night. On a full moon night, there's always a hormonal change inside us, which affects our fertility cycle. That is, we tend to ovulate. I'm sure I must have been a very, very horny soul that night. That's why we don't come out during a lunar cycle. It's not safe for us and for those around us."

"Well, that explains it." I nod and heave a sigh. "You smelled a little different that night. Almost like you were—"

"In heat."

"Yes! I thought you were in heat and it was your heat pheromones that were making me lose my hold on myself. I kept thinking your heat was forcing me into rut."

"No, I definitely wasn't in heat. It wasn't my time. It was the full-moon's effect. Lunar cycle always changes something inside the squirrel shifters. Our behavior is more unusual and aggressive when we are exposed to a full moon."

"Then why did you come out that day?"

He knew what would happen if he exposed himself to the moon, yet he came out. I growl my frustration, and saw my jaw back and forth.

"Hey, it was cloudy, and the moon wasn't visible. It was hidden nicely, so I didn't think any harm would come as long as it was concealed. Unfortunately, that didn't happen?"

"You think?"

"I know, I know, I'm sorry. I'll be careful next time. Promise."

"You need to make that promise to yourself. What if you were out with someone else? Things could have been much worse."

"Like they are not already."

I narrow my eyes and scoot back, then hoist myself up.

Oscar scrambles and stands up as well. "So what now?"

"Now nothing."

"Nothing? But—"

"I'll work on the menu tonight. And I promise to respond to your emails and call. I won't avoid you."

"That's it?"

"What else do you expect?"

His nostrils flare, eyes blazing with fire and rage. "I expect you to acknowledge that we fucked on Halloween night. And that there might be a baby or babies inside me."

"W-what?" I gasp, my hand flying to the chest. "B-babies?" I shuffle back a step or two. "But... but... you said you weren't in heat that night, so the chances of you getting pregnant is one in a million."

He face palms and shakes his head, eyes closing tightly. He exhales a sigh and opens his eyes, then looks into my eyes. "I said I might be, I didn't say I was. Read my words."

"Then why the hell would you say you might have a baby or babies in you?"

"Dear gods, I said there's a chance. A chance. Like zero point zero, zero, nine percentage. Which means zero to nil."

"Aarrrgh," I pull my hair, and fulminate some very colorful words inside my head that would have a nun covering her ears. "So you are not pregnant?"

"I don't know." He shrugs his shoulders, a bored expression on his face.

I will throttle him.

"You either are, or you are not!" I shout, my chest heaving.

"Well, I haven't found out," he snaps. "When I do I will let you know."

I grind my teeth, clench my hands into fists at my sides, then release them, and heave a shuddering breath.

I'm okay.

I'm not angry.

I can handle this.

"Will you please find out whether you are pregnant or not?"

"Since you asked so nicely, I will tomorrow," he says sweetly. What is he up to now? What plan is he concocting inside that massive brain of his?

"Would you like to come?"

"I can't." No way I'm going to a hospital with him.

"You should come, you know. Satisfy that curiosity I know is lurking inside you."

"We'll see."

"Okay." His grins like he's got me on the hook, his eyes shimmering with amusement. "Talk to you tomorrow."

What is he up to now?

CHAPTER 7

OSCAR

I know I shouldn't have egged him on so much, but in the several weeks since we haven't spoken—more like he refused to talk to me in any form—I have realized I'm attracted to him.

Just attracted, and nothing else.

I mean, the man pisses me off. Most of the time I want to strangle him, like the last few weeks when he wouldn't meet me, or take my calls, or reply to my emails. All those times I wanted to choke him to death and slap him senseless.

It has been hell to concentrate on anything except for what transpired in the forest between us.

I have snapped and cursed in front of other people so many times, I'm ashamed to say I don't care about my image anymore.

Fuck image. See I'm cursing. This is what has become of me since meeting that man. I cuss and call names.

Gah!

I should get back to work, the one I have been neglecting the last couple of weeks, but I'm thinking of Finnick and what I did in the forest. I can't forget about it. Trust me, I have tried.

It has been hard to accept in my heart that I jumped him in the forest. My mind knows I didn't have any control and that Finnick did what he did because my pheromones incentivized his Alpha appetency, but my heart has been wailing inside, weeping with regret and shame.

I have been trying to talk to him after running away like a coward, leaving him naked in the forest.

I thought he was disgusted or angry at me for molesting him like a high as a kite whore, rubbing and grinding against him.

I never expected him to be so understanding, and to hear that's all it'll be between us, a mistake, that stings a lot more than a safety pin this morning.

I rub my arm and mutter under my breath, "It's okay. So what if he doesn't want to take things further. I'll convince him to be my friend."

And he really needs someone in his life. I can't fathom what it must be like to live with so much pain and sorrow, and to keep moving with life.

But has he actually moved on with his life? I don't think so. I shake my head. Not really, no.

He stays alone, doesn't visit anyone, won't attend any social gatherings, always snaps and growls. And there's a darkness in his eyes, an empty ocean without life.

I make a frustrated noise for the way he's living his life in solitude.

He's so angry all the time.

I ache for him, for his disconsolateness.

I want to turn back and hug him. Hug him for all the years he's been alone, he suffered in silence, for the anguish and rage building inside him.

For the lost love and his spark.

No wonder Rosemary won't leave him alone. She knows he's hurting and is miserable. That he needs a gentle hand and lots and lots of attention and love. Which she is giving him whenever he is allowing her. Be it bickering, or visiting him uninvited.

I love that woman for just caring about him. She won't give up on him, I know it. That is why she is putting so much effort into my little project.

When I had said I wanted to host a thank-you party for the town residents, she muttered something under breath. I can't remember her exact words, because I know they were not meant for my ears, but I was still able to catch a few things.

She said something like 'this will force him to talk' and 'come out of his dark shell'.

Now I know what she meant then.

Finnick's heart is closed, it's locked and shoved deep down somewhere he doesn't want to reach, doesn't want to feel. And I understand after that kind of tragedy, and what he has witnessed, anybody would keep themselves from feeling. From letting someone in, fearing it'll be snatched again.

But that's life. It giveth and it taketh away.

However, I have decided to bring him out of his dark hole, and I know we'll be butting heads. A lot. And will curse each other as well, but I'm not going to back down from this challenge.

I'm going to convince him—force him—to be my friend. I don't care what he has to say, he's going to be my friend before Thanksgiving.

I reach the corner of his street, but stop when I hear my name being called.

"Oscar!"

I look over my shoulder.

It's Finnick, running toward me.

I blink and my heart suddenly soars. I spin on my heel and cock my head.

"Are you deaf?" He bends at the waist and rests his hands on his thighs, panting, wheezing between breaths. His face is flushed and sweaty.

"Huh?"

"I have called you at least five or six times."

"I didn't hear you."

"Obvi... ously," he stretches the word between his puffing. He straightens, and takes in a big gulp of air, filling his lungs, then blows out. He repeats the process two more times, then meets my gaze with narrowed eyes. "What do you think you are doing?"

Huh? What am I doing? "Nothing. Just walking home. Why?"

"Are you out of your gods-damned mind?" He shouts, resting his hands on his hips. "Are you that daft?"

I cringe and take a step back. "Stop shouting. You'll wake people."

"Someone should witness your stupidity other than me. My gods, how can you be so stupid?"

Okay, that's it. Who the hell does he think he is to call me stupid. "What's your problem, haan? Why are you shouting?"

"You are my problem. You," he grits the word like it's poison.

"What the hell have I done to you? Why are you always angry with me? Is it because I'm an omega?" I plant my hands on my hips and pull back my shoulders. "Seriously, what's your deal? Can't you talk to me politely like a sane person? I'm not a child for you to treat me like one."

"Then stop behaving like one." I open my mouth to argue, but he stops me with a raised hand. "You know it's not safe to walk alone this late at night, yet you are. If that's not stupid then what is? Getting kidnapped, or maybe being attacked by a feral animal? You should know an omega should always be careful."

"This is Vale Valley, Finnick. It is the safest place on earth. The town's magic protects us all. It won't let a deranged man or animal in."

"No place is safe for an omega, Oscar. No place. You don't know what's lurking in the shadows."

"It's safe to walk in this town. I have taken so many midnight walks, and not once was I attacked. Nothing has happened to me. This town is protected by magic." I twist and turn my body to show him. "See? Nothing has happened to me. It's safe. I'm safe."

"Whatever. Where's your fucking car?" he snaps

Gods, if he doesn't stop with that snappish tone of his, I'm going to smack him upside down. I've had enough of his waspish attitude to last a lifetime.

"Where is it?" he growls, then grabs my shoulders and shakes me, which bugs the hell out of me.

"I left it at home," I snap, bristling, baring my teeth.

"Why the hell, damn it!"

"Because I wanted to walk and clear my head, but somehow my legs brought me to you," I spat.

With a frustrated sigh, he pulls his hair. "Come, I'll walk you home."

"You don't need to do that. I can walk home by myself perfectly fine."

"I want to. It'll give me some peace of mind to know you have reached home safely, and that is possible only when I will see it with my own eyes." He lifts his chin, a determined look enters his eyes.

I narrow my eyes, ready to argue, but huff and give up. There's no point in arguing with him. He won't budge.

I just know it. He's in that Alphahole mode, all growly and demanding.

Pulling my shoulders back, I spin on my heel, and mutter, "Fine. Follow me then."

I walk briskly, my shoulder blades aching from so much tension inside me. And the thick silence between us is getting on my nerves. No words are passed, no looks are exchanged. Just silence.

I don't understand this man and his strange Alpha ways.

One moment he can be charming, playful, and the next he'll be in a shouting contest.

I look at him out of the corner of my eyes, and find him looking around, body relaxed, steps easy, face calm, but his eyes are as sharp as a cheetah's, ready to catch and pound any interloper that might come into his line of vision.

Aah, trying to be macho. Like that will scare anyone.

I snort, which snaps his gaze at me. I shrug my right shoulder and ignore him.

He growls, breathing heavily.

That growly noise he makes every time grates my nerves, and not the kind where I want to cover my ears, but the kind that sends my blood rushing.

The kind that has my heart thundering.

The kind that makes my knees buckle.

Whatever.

So Finnick affects me sexually. Big deal. Nothing wrong with that, but I know we are kind of frenemies—no, not that. We are definitely not friends, yet, and we definitely are not enemies, yet.

I don't know what we are, but most of the time when he's around me, and opens that mouth of his, I want to thump him.

I know there will come a day when I will finally give in to my urges to hit him, and I look forward to that day.

It's coming soon.

You just wait, Mr. Finnick Grooch. You just wait.

As the gust of a wind blows, chills fill deep into my bones. I rub my arms, cursing myself for forgetting my jacket at home.

This man, he made me forget my jacket. Gods above, he makes me forget everything.

Like now. The way he's making that noise at the back of his throat, like he's humming a tune. It is sending a delicious thrill through my veins.

Increasing my pace, I put some distance between us. I don't want to hear him droning out some melody. He's not good. Not at all. He sings horrendously. And his voice is meh.

Liar.

Whatever.

How the hell can he bombinate a jingle after spoiling my night? Why is he crooning?

Maybe he's enjoying the rift of strain stretching between us. Enjoying showing me who's the boss.

In your dreams!

Why can't he be sweet like the guys I like to date? Why can't he talk to me with civility? What is it about me that makes him want to take a step back? Why can't he lo—

Don't go there, Oscar. Don't go.

Right.

He's not capable of doing it. He won't let anyone into his heart.

I clench my hands into fists at my sides and have a ted talk with my heart about boundaries, and expectations, and Finnick.

I remind it about the rejection, about his dismissal of us.

No matter is worth begging for affection and acceptance. It should be given freely, not begged for.

I look over my shoulder and see he has caught up with me. He smirks and whistles, walking leisurely and still keeping up with my fast strides.

As soon as we reach my house, I open the gate and get inside, immediately closing it, blocking Finnick's entry. "Thank you for seeing me home. I'll see you tomorrow," I say and run up the steps, and quickly open the door I know my parents must keep unlocked for me.

"No you won't." I hear him shout, but don't turn around to answer him.

I get inside and close the door, then lean slumped against it.

His words pull a smile on my lips.

We'll see about that. Mr. Grooch. We'll see.

"Oscar, honey, is that you?" Mama calls from the kitchen as I'm removing my shoes.

"Yes, Mama, it's me." I walk toward her. "What are you doing awake at this time? Why aren't you asleep?" I ask her and take a seat next to her at the kitchen island.

"I couldn't sleep, and you went out pretty late." She shrugs her shoulders. She's holding a teacup in her palm, steam wafting from it.

"You didn't have to wait for me."

"I know I don't have to, but a mother's heart will always worry knowing her baby is out late at night."

"Oh, Mama, I'm a big boy. I can take care of myself.

"You'll always be my baby. You'll understand a parent's heart and worry over their children when you have some of your own."

"This is Vale Valley. Our town is the safest place on earth. It is protected by magic."

"No place is safe, Oscar. Every wall is penetrable, every magic can be undone."

This is the second time I have heard that phrase, and it's scares the hell out of me.

I don't like it when people say our town is not safe, because it is the safest. I know it in my heart, and the witches' coven make sure to keep it that way as well.

"Well, ours is," I snap, and regret it immediately.

What is wrong with me? Why am I getting angry at her?

Maybe I should just call it a night. Today has been a rough day. Very stressful. I'm not thinking straight right now.

"Sorry, Mama."

"It's alright." She pats my hand, then squeezes it for emphasis. I look down at her hand still holding mine, and wonder if that's how I'll feel if I find out I'm pregnant with Finnick's baby tomorrow.

"I'm going to go to sleep now that I know you are safe and at home. See you in the morning. Love you."

"Love you too, Mama. Good night."

"Good night."

I head to my room and change into my nightclothes, then freshen up and climb into my bed.

I open the hospital app, and book an appointment for tomorrow morning.

I'm dreading it… how I will feel if I find out I'm pregnant.

Will I resent the baby? Of course not, it's not the baby's fault. I was the foolish one who ventured out on a full-moon night.

I'm not sure what I should pray about tonight, but I ask the only thing I'm capable of asking right now.

Please make everything alright.

CHAPTER 8

FINNICK

I have tossed and turned all night. All fucking night. I haven't gotten sleep worth a wink, and it's already morning.

It's going to be one of those days, you know. One where I'm even more snappish and grumpy than I am usually.

My kitchen staff will have a wonderful day.

Fabulous.

I groan and get off the bed, and take care of my business and brush my teeth. After wearing my running clothes and shoes, I grab my mp3 player and house keys, then go out.

I push the wireless earbuds into my ears and blast the music on.

My feet pound on the pavement, heart beating, pulse spiking with every step I take.

And my thoughts run back to Oscar.

Ugh.

Why is he always on my mind? Why?

Oscar has somehow managed to get under my skin, and fast.

What is it about him that makes my heart clench then

jump with jubilation? My head always circles back to him. Always.

I shouldn't have agreed to cater his event, then gone for a walk on Halloween night.

And now he might be pregnant with my baby.

This can't be happening.

What will I do if he is actually pregnant? Am I going to abandon the baby and him? Break all ties and move out of town? Go start somewhere else?

I can't do that. I can't have them fend for themselves, but I also don't know if I can live with them. More importantly I don't want to mate with Oscar.

Unfortunately, if I don't, then my child will be called a bastard. And that is unacceptable.

"Arrgh." I push myself and increase my pace, my breath comes out in puffs, chilled air piercing my heated skin.

The sun is out and smiling. I feel like he is smirking at me, at my misery.

Well, fuck you, sun. Not everyone can be happy and shiny like you.

It gleams, shimmering more, as if to say, 'I know'.

Whatever.

I finish my three-mile run and head back home.

As soon as I'm inside the house, I drop the key and mp3 player and wireless earbuds into the bowl and head toward the kitchen.

I hear my cellphone buzzing in the living room.

I swiftly grab a bottle of water and a bottle of Gatorade from the fridge, and head out.

My cellphone beeps again.

I place the bottles on the coffee table and grab my cellphone.

As I power it on, I see three notifications from Oscar. One Email and two messages.

I open the email first thinking it might be work related.

FROM: Oscar Nutter
To: Finnick Sethi
Subject: Do you want to come for my appointment?
The appointment is scheduled for 8 am. Bring me some breakfast, okay?
Chao.
Xoxo
Oscar.

THAT BRAT!

I should spank his behind with a paddle, then gag that smart ass mouth of his. That'll teach him not to sass me.

I snort and remember this is Oscar, and nothing will shut him up. Nothing.

Only my cock inside his mouth.

Fuck no! That is not happening again. I order my brain to banish that image and thought. It doesn't have any place in my fucked-up life right.

I blow out a frustrated sigh and open his text message then.

Oscar: *Hey, so do you wanna know if I'm carrying your spawn or not? The doctor's appointment is at 8 a.m. Bring me snacks, I'm craving tacos!*

Oscar: *Oh, and some freshly made orange juice please. I have heard orange is good for the little seed in my tummy.*

Gods, this boy!

I have been telling him since last night I won't join him for the doctor's appointment. But it's like he can't hear me at all. I respond to his email quickly.

. . .

FROM: Finnick Sethi

To: Oscar Nutter

Subject: Re: Do you want to come or my appointment?

I said I'm not coming last night. And go eat in the hospital cafeteria.

I DON'T BOTHER with pleasantries, and just send the email. Then next, I respond to his text message.

Me: Sorry, can't come. Not making tacos today. Look for someone else to buy you snacks. And stop messaging.

I drop my cellphone next to me and pick up the Gatorade and drain it in a few gulps.

FROM: Oscar Nutter

To: Finnick Sethi

Subject: Re: Do you want to come for my appointment?

That's not how you should be treating me and the little bean in my belly. I'm hurt. He's hurt! And cafeteria food is yuck! I want you to cook for me. What's the point of becoming a chef if you cannot cook for peanut?

(NO KISSES and hugs for you)

Spawn-carrying Oscar.

UGH. Now he's guilt shaming me. This boy knows how to twist my own words and feed me.

I should stay firm on my decision.

Do not waver.

Do not waver.

Do not waver.

But what if he needs me, or something is wrong with him?

And what if he gives me the wrong report, or lies to me?

Nothing is stopping him from blackmailing me.

I read the email once more and gnash my teeth when I reach the part he's talking about the baby.

My heart warms at the word, and its different variations Oscar is using to make a light of this, but there is an unbearable ache inside my chest. Ache for all that's lost and cannot be found again.

Incorrect!

I ignore those syllables and reroute my head to think about something else.

Another email pops up from Oscar, and I close my eyes. Unsure if I should open it or ignore it.

Before I can make a decision, my finger clicks on the freshly arrived email and it snaps open.

From: Oscar Nutter

To: Finnick Sethi

Subject: Re: Do you want to come for my appointment?

Please come?

#

#

#

#

So I can act as la demoiselle en détresse ;)

Muahahaha!!! (Evil laugh emoji)

I'm going to choke him to death. I'm ready to staple that mouth of his—more like his finger—for saying such irritating things.

For a second there, I was actually thinking of going with him for the doctor's appointment, until I read the next line after several spaces.

Dear gods, this man will be the death of me.

Another email arrives and I know it's from him.

I should ignore it. I really should ignore this one and just focus on getting ready for work. However, my fingers itch to click on it and read it.

No, I will not distress myself for the likes of him. It's time I stop entertaining him.

And with that thought, I lock my cellphone and throw it on the sofa, collect the water bottle and head toward my bedroom.

IT TAKES me nearly twenty minutes to get ready for work.

I check all the stuff I need before leaving the house.

Wallet? I pat my pants pocket. Check.

Banana? In my hand. Check.

Coffee? Travel mug is filled and ready to be consumed. Check.

Keys? Dangling between my fingers. Check.

Cellphone? In my pocket. Check

I'm ready to leave.

I unlock the car with the fob, open the door and sit behind the wheels.

I take a calming breath to center myself, then start the car.

Today will be a better day.

No new event can spoil it.

Except for one.

My staff is already here. We open at seven in the morning to serve a mini breakfast platter. Which is always handled by my Chef de Partie and Comis Chef, that is, Velinda and Clancy.

The Chef's Corner mostly focuses on serving lunch and dinner, but our breakfast hours are just as busy as the lunch and dinnertime are.

I head into my office and think about what to cook for today's special. I don't like repeating dishes. Anything special I make and offer to customers is not repeated for a few months. Most specials are expensive stuff, or something new I want to try and later offer it for online ordering only.

I can't change the paper menu everyday now, can I? Fortunately for me, it is very easy to do on the restaurant website. I love technological evolution, but I hate it as well. I like the dependency I have over it.

One of the business strategies I have learned over the years working in various countries and restaurants.

I work in silence, this time devoted to just me. No one will disturb me—

My cellphone vibrates on the table, and my gaze rolls toward it. I see an email notification from Oscar.

I puff out the air from my lungs and close my eyes, asking the gods for some—okay, a lot of—patience to deal with him and his antics.

Only he has the nerve to disturb me at this time. Only him.

Noise… at the back of my throat vibrates, and I drop the pen in my hand onto the table, then snatch the device and unlock it, clicking the email open. After filling my lungs with air, I read it.

From: Oscar Nutter

To: Finnick Sethi

Subject: Re: Do you want to come for my appointment?

The results are in! I'm pregnant! You are going to be a daddy

MY HEART about stops and I feel an intense jolt rush through me.

Feeling light-headed, I rest my head on the table, clench my hand into fists.

Dear gods!

He's pregnant. I'm going to be a father, again.

Fuck!

Nausea rolls deep in the pit of my stomach, the bile coming up, up, up.

I bolt out of my chair and run toward the small bathroom I have attached to my office, and empty the contents of my stomach into the toilet.

My eyes water, nose tingles insistently, and body tenses, coiling tight, shrinking like soup boiling in a pan as more stuff, gods only know from where, comes out.

I heave, and heave, and heave!

Finally, I rest my forehead against the rim of the toilet and just sit.

Tears well in my eyes, and I do nothing to stop them. I just cry, my body shaking, air in my lungs shuddering.

Everything aches in my body. My heart, my head, my soul.

A baby. Another baby.

Images of Rohan's snort giggle, his smile, his babbling come to the forefront of my mind, filling me with longing to hold him, to have him one more time in my arms.

I would give anything, anything to have my family back with me for just five minutes.

I miss them. I miss them so much.

When will the grief and the throbbing in my chest ever go away? When?

Why can't I forget them? Why?

I scoot back and rest against the wall, pulling my knees to my chest.

The past is meant to shape the present and the future. Nani's words rattle in my head. *Some souls are meant to go early to pan a new future for the rest of us.*

Who gave anyone the right to decide how the future should be carved? To take away our loved ones, to scour one's soul?

Life is nothing but a Pandora's box, full of mysteries and anomalies. Don't question it, accept it.

I will never accept merciless killing. I will never accept the death of my family.

Let go, my love. Let go and live. Misha's melodious voice glides through the fog of memories coming back to me.

It has been so long, years, since I have heard his voice whisper in my head. I miss him, his wisdom, and patience, and empathetic heart.

Why haven't I heard his voice all these years?

Because you shut me out.

Those words are like a punch to my chest, piercing my heart like a poison dagger. I didn't mean to. But the last image of him, ripped open, bleeding in our front yard, is the one that has taken root in my mind, in my memories.

A shudder rakes through me, my heart shrinks from the assault of all the caches of the past.

A sob rips from my throat, and all the suppressed emotions come out after being dormant for years.

My heartache.

My loneliness.

My exhaustion from holding everything inside me.

I cover my face and cry, shedding the remnants of the past. I weep and let my heart open for the loss. I sob and let my body embrace all the emotions I have been holding inside, suppressing them for years. I'm feeling too much. *Too much.* And yet, a numbness seeps into every cell of my being.

Let go, my love. Let go and live. Feel, Finnick.

"I-I-I don't know how t-to do t-tha-t," I sob, and wrap my arms around my knees, rest my cheek against them, and rock back and forth, my shoulders shaking.

You can do it.

I don't think I can.

You can do it.

I don't know if I want to.

You can do it.

Don't want to let go.

You can do it.

I'm afraid of forgetting everyone.

You can do it.

I'm afraid of happiness. I'm afraid Misha will resent me for finding joy again in life. I'm afraid Misha is already begrudging me from the afterlife for even surviving the massacre.

Do you really think he's that shallow? My heart questions.

No. He was the most giving, selfless person. I'm one hundred percent sure, Misha must be cursing me right now, calling me all sorts of names from the afterlife for acting like a pigheaded lurdan.

I'm sorry, love. I can't do it. I just can't

Can't or won't, Fin? Don't punish yourself. It was not your fault. You can't protect everyone. You are not superhuman. You are a human, meant to live and die. Meant to feel and function. Meant to love and cry.

I know what I am. I know what I'm capable of, and my

heart is not strong enough to love again. It is not inclined to love another soul. It is not open to experience loss again.

That's a coward's way to live, and you are no coward.

Loss makes any man a coward, and I accept my cowardice.

Let go and love again, Finnick. For me, for Rohan. Live. Really live!

I ignore those words and heave myself up, then stand on trembling legs. Inhaling a shuddering breath, I walk toward the sink on dead jelly legs and wash my hands and rinse out my mouth.

As the water washes away the events of the morning, I wonder if I'm strong enough to move on and do as Misha asks of me.

Only one way to find out.

CHAPTER 9

OSCAR

When Finnick doesn't respond to my email immediately, I give him five minutes as a buffer. And when he doesn't reply back after the five-minute buffer, I send him a few texts. No responses for any of them.

That means three things. He is either ignoring me, or maybe he knows I'm joking and doesn't want to encourage my foolishness, or something is wrong.

And it's the "something wrong" part that my brain has latched on to.

I thank the nurse at the station and get out of the hospital, and jog toward my car.

An itch takes root in the pit of my stomach, aloofly rising, spreading into other parts of my body.

It's a warning. I know it is.

My body begs me to see him, and I know I have to follow my instincts, and find out what is wrong.

I get in and start the car and drive toward The Chef's Corner. I have to see him with my own eyes, and make sure he's okay.

I run my fingers through my hair and make a frustrated

noise in the back of my throat when the car in front of me slows down, then stops altogether, parking haphazardly half on the curb and the other half on the highway.

What the fuck? This is not a parking place.

I punch my steering wheel and curse the owner of the car for being so careless.

Don't they know how to park? And where to park?

Shame slaps me hard as I watch an elderly lady come out of the car and rush around to the passenger side.

She opens the door and helps an elderly man out and he pukes on the side.

Shit!

I get out of the car and rush toward them. "Is he okay? What happened?"

Their scent fills my nose. Humans.

"We are fine dear," the woman says, sadness shimmering in her eyes. "It's the side effects of his chemo. He'll be fine in a few minutes."

Gods, the pesky demonic disease, it ravishes and defiles any soul it can find. No one is immune to it. Not one soul on this planet.

"Do you need any help? Want me to drop you guys home? Or call someone for you?"

"If you wouldn't mind, can you call my son, Landon, from my cell phone? It's on the console and number four in emergency contacts is his number."

"Sure can do." I rush toward the driver's seat and grab her cellphone from the console, then press the number four and the call goes through.

I inform their son, Landon, about the situation and where we are currently, and ask him to come immediately.

I wait with the elderly couple until their son arrives.

Once he's here I get back in my car and drive toward Finnick.

It takes me less than ten minutes to reach the diner. I find a spot and quickly park my car and walk inside the diner.

I wave to Dina and walk toward Finnick's office.

"You don't wanna go there. He doesn't like being disturbed at this time," Dina shouts.

"He doesn't like being disturbed any time," I say over my shoulder, and hear the patrons chuckle.

I knock on the door when I reach his office. No answer.

Okay then. I knock again. Still no answer.

The seed of unease intensifies in my stomach, sending a sour taste into my mouth.

I know it's rude to enter someone's room, or house uninvited, but right now, I need to know he's alright. So, without knocking, without announcing myself, I open the door and enter.

The office is empty. I mean, Finnick is not there.

I hear a water tap being run somewhere. As I move in and close the door behind me, then follow the noise coming from behind a door on the right side of the room.

When the water tap shuts off, I hold my breath and wait for him.

The door opens slowly, and a figure comes out.

Finnick.

His eyes are bloodshot and swollen, his face flushed and pale. What tugs at my heart is the defeated sag of his shoulders.

What has happened?

Is it because of me? Have I done this?

Our gazes connect, and there's so much sorrow and clarity in his eyes that hasn't been there since I met him all those weeks ago.

There's no anger as well.

"What happened?" I walk toward him.

"Nothing," he says softly. "Just something I should have dealt with a long time ago, but haven't."

He makes no sense. No sense at all.

"What?" I cock my head and wait for him to explain.

"Nothing. It's nothing." He walks toward me and stands awkwardly in front of me. "What did the doctor say? Are you okay? Is the baby okay?"

Shit! Yeah, I totally forgot about that.

"About that." I rub the back of my neck, biting my lips, and avert from looking into his eyes. "I lied about being pregnant."

"Huh?"

"In my defense, I was just trying to pull your leg, and simply rile you. In fact, I emailed you again saying I was only joking and it's not true. I'm not pregnant, not carrying your spawn."

"You are not pregnant?" His face falls, and he stares down at his hands, then his gaze moves and stays on my abdomen.

Huh. Is that disappointment I see on his face?

But... but... he said he doesn't want to have a family, doesn't want to love again, open his heart and all the grief from loss nonsense. And now he's disheartened that I'm not pregnant.

I don't understand this man. His moods, his behavior, his emotions, they give me whiplash.

"No, I'm not."

"Oh." That felt like a monotone voice, it breaks something inside me, then rebuilds.

Hope.

Hope, that he wants something, anything from me.

"Did you want me to be?" I hold my breath and wait, my heart pounding inside my chest.

He nods and looks up and meets my gaze, his eyes shimmering with a small smile.

"You really, really wanted me to be pregnant?"

"Yeah I really, really wanted you to be pregnant." He smiles.

I search his eyes, they are light, but there's still some residual pain after the words have been said.

"But you said you didn't want to—"

"I know. That was my grief talking. But after reading your email and knowing you were carrying my baby… let's just say I finally dealt with what I had locked inside me for years."

"And what's that?"

"My emotions, my heart, my loss. More importantly, my guilt for surviving."

"So many things? You had to deal with so many things?"

He bows his head in answer. "I had shut down after losing my family and the whole cete, locked my emotions, but let one fester inside me. Guilt." He looks down and laces his fingers. "I still don't understand how I could have survived and others didn't. It has been eating me day and night for the last eight years."

"But you said some of your cete members made it."

"Yeah, but they were all harmed, and I was not. I barely had a scratch on me."

"Were you there when your cete was being attacked?"

"I arrived late. Too late. I was at work when it started, but that day I'd left work early to surprise my pregnant mate and child. When I arrived, it was almost over. The house was full of blood and bodies. One hyena attacked me, but I fought back and killed it."

"So you survived after fighting valiantly and others didn't."

"Yes."

"And thank the gods for that." His gaze snaps and meets mine. I smile and cup his cheek . "You survived, because you were meant to. It was fate. And because you freaking survived, I would have been pregnant today—which I'm not —but I would have been if the test result had come positive."

He shrugs his shoulders. "I don't know about that."

"But I do. Was the death of your family necessary? I don't think so. It could have been avoided if Fate wanted it, but it didn't. And because it happened, you came to Vale Valley. And to me."

"To you, huh?" He smirks.

"Yup to me." I drop my hand and step back. "You have been meant to meet me, to be my friend."

"But what if I want to be your lover?" He throws the question out carelessly.

My jaw drops, hitting the floor with a loud, resounding thud, that I'm sure is matching the beat of my heart. I blink and look at him dazed.

Has he just said what I think he just said?

"Will you have me? As your lover I mean?"

Yep, he has.

Dear gods, I can't believe this.

I slap a hand against my cheek, then the other. I slap my cheeks with both hands once more, unable to accept and convince myself that it's real.

It can't be.

I'm hallucinating, or maybe dreaming. Or maybe I have had too much coffee.

I should lay off that stuff. Mama has been telling me for years now to stop drinking so much coffee. 'It'll rearrange your brain' she says. And maybe that is what is happening now? My brain has finally given up and I'm losing my mind.

"Say something?"

"What?" I look into his eyes.

The vulnerability in his eyes snaps me out of my stupor.

"Do you want me as your lover, Oscar? You asked me yesterday why I can't open my heart, and I gave you my reasons. But after thinking it through, I know I want to try and move on with my life. I have only been existing, walking aimlessly, with no destination and goal, but I want to change that. I want to *live*."

My heart feels full. So full, I'm afraid it will explode. His words bring tears to my eyes, and my lips wobble.

"I want to love, and let love in. So, will you have me? Will you let me be your Alpha?" He cocks his head to the side, a small smile still playing on his lips.

"Yes." The word is out and I don't regret it. Not one bit.

I know I said last night it doesn't matter if we aren't together as lovers, but I lied.

I want him more than anything I have ever dreamed of.

I wrap my arms around his neck and jump on him, wrapping my legs around his hips and hugging him tight.

"Well, aren't you excited." Finnick laughs, his shoulders shaking.

I pull back and look into his eyes. "I am. I'm so excited and happy. I was hoping things would change between us, but I didn't expect them to change so soon."

"I know I have done a one eighty in like a few hours, but I had this epiphany that I haven't honored the dead by not embracing life. And Misha put some sense into me."

"Who's Misha?" I cannot help but growl.

"My mate." I narrow my eyes, nostrils flaring. "My dead mate." He corrects his words.

And then it hits me. He has spoken to his dead mate? How?

"Um, Finnick, you cannot talk to the dead, like at all. Unless you are a witch and a medium."

"I'm neither of those. But I do hear my mate's voice sometimes."

Something like jealousy slithers through my veins when he refers to his dead mate as a living being. My animal doesn't like it, which is ridiculous. His mate is dead and cannot come between us, but that doesn't stop my heart from fearing that Finnick can be taken away from me.

"Sorry, it'll take some time to get used to saying my dead mate instead of mate."

"How about you just use his name? My animal… doesn't like it when you refer to him like he's still alive."

"Okay, I can do that."

"Thank you." I peck him on the lips. "Now let's make some things very clear. I do not share. Like at all. I don't like being lied to. I am not a morning person. I don't believe in exercise, but I love meditating and doing yoga—which I don't consider to be a form of exercise. I still live with my parents, as do my siblings. That's just how we squirrels roll. I earn my keep and I have saved a lot of money, but it's mine to use and spend however I see fit. Which means, if I want to buy you something… I will."

"Okay." He inclines his head, eyes shimmering with wicked amusement.

I haven't seen him like this, so carefree, openly displaying his emotions. There's no rage, no resentment, no guilt, only some lingering sadness and pain, which I'm sure will vanish eventually.

His mouth curves and his whole face lights up.

I become a puddle of goo. The man's got charm. "Now, your turn."

"What do you want to know?"

"Anything and everything."

"Okay. Let's sit on the sofa and talk. You are too heavy." I smack him on the head, which only makes him laugh. "I am not heavy."

"If you say so." He grins, and drops me on the sofa.

I bounce a little, but settle down. "Okay, now tell me."

"Well, I'm a morning person. I like to run. On my day off,

I like to watch documentaries and cookery shows. I also enjoy good action, thriller movies. Love reading books, fiction, any genre will do. Love cooking, prefer healthy food to greasy food."

"Ugh, this cannot work between us. I love greasy food. I love anything that is unhealthy for the body. I don't like eating grass like some people do."

"Who said anything about eating grass? I said I like eating healthy food. I eat steak, and meat and seafood. I just don't fill my stomach with junk food."

"This definitely will not work. I just know it."

"Don't you know opposites attract?"

"I do, but that doesn't mean a lick when you cannot eat what I like."

"We'll see about that." His eyes gleam with concealed amusement.

I narrow my eyes and punch him on the shoulder.

"So violent," he says, rubbing his shoulder.

"You bring it out of me."

"I have that effect on people." He raises his chin and thrust out his chest, eyes gleaming—more like laughing.

I roll my eyes. "Don't I know it."

He pulls me into his arms and we sit in a comfortable silence.

I look up into his eyes and ask, "We are really doing this?"

"We are really doing this."

CHAPTER 10

I'm meeting Finnick today to discuss the menu he's prepared for the event. I'm excited to see what he's planned for the guests to eat.

And I'm thinking of inviting him for the Thanksgiving lunch at my place. I'm nervous about it. Not sure how he'll react, or if he'll accept the invitation. I've already informed my parents I'm inviting him. They know who he is and I have told them a glazed version about his life.

They are happy for me.

In a few days' time, he's become to mean so much more to me than I've ever thought is possible.

I'm waiting for him at Grady's, an Irish pub owned by Frank Andrews. It is across the street from the community center.

I order a beer and some French fries until he arrives.

He told me lunch hours are busy for The Chef's Corner like any other restaurant in town. It is impossible to leave a packed diner.

I told him to meet me after the lunch-hour rush.

It is past three. He'll be here anytime now.

The pub's door opens and a frazzled-looking Finnick barrels in with a bag in his hand.

I wave my hand and get his attention.

His eyes light when our gazes connect, his lips curving into that half smile I have come to love so much.

He walks toward me, all smooth and light.

He takes the seat opposite me and drops the bag onto the empty seat next to him.

"What's in that?" I jerk my chin toward the bag.

"Something for you and your family."

"Oh, what?"

"Today's special."

"What was today's special?"

"You can find out after you reach home." He smirks and signals for the waitress to come.

"What can I get you?" the waitress asks.

"I'll have a glass of beer, whatever's on the tap, and a cheese burger, please."

She nods and turns on her heels.

"Please tell me," I show him my puppy-dog eyes, batting them for effect.

He leans forward and motions for me to come forward too. I do and wait for him to tell me, but the bastard only kisses my cheek. "You can wait for a few more hours to find out."

"But I don't want to wait till I reach home. I wanna know now."

"Patience is a virtue."

I huff and lean back, then cross my arms over my chest. "Fine, don't tell me."

He cocks his head, the smile still stretching his lips. "You'll love what's in there." He points his thumb at the bag.

"Overconfident much?" I cock my right brow at him.

"I know my skills and ability." He raises his brow as well.

"Whatever."

He laughs, and bumps his knee with mine. "Come on, tell me how your day has been so far."

"It has been productive. I have detailed out the stage decoration, and seating arrangements, and ordered the materials I'll need to pretty the center."

"That's wonderful. What about the space for dancing? Did you figure it out where you are going to arrange for it?"

I remove the design of the event and show him what I'm thinking about. He likes all my ideas, which pleases me immensely.

"You have given a lot of thought about this haven't you?" he asks.

"I have." I play footsie with him as I explain to him about this event. "It's something I have been thinking about for almost a year now. I had wanted to do it sooner, but I have been swamped with so many events, that I didn't find any time to do it sooner. So, I made sure I keep myself free of any events for the whole month of December. That way I can concentrate only on this."

"You'll do a brilliant job, and people will love it. What you are doing is very generous."

"This town has given me so much, Finnick. Happiness, a business to run and flourish, and stay close to my family... And you." The last two words come out softer. "So I'm thankful for a lot more things. Things that still haven't happened yet, but I know they will."

I leave it at that, letting him decide the implication of my words.

His eyes and face soften. "I'm thankful too. For the present and the future that I know I will find here."

The words *with you* are unsaid—by both of us.

His beer and food arrives. "You didn't order anything for yourself?" Finnick asks me.

"I had an early lunch with my parents, so I'm not hungry."

"Do you want to share this with me?" He points to his burger.

"No, you eat. I have this." I point to my French fries.

"Okay." He takes a sip of his beer, then a bite of his burger. "Let me show you what I have decided for the event's menu." He removes a paper from the bag and hands it to me.

"I don't want to serve food that people are familiar with, so I have chosen three cuisines. Thai, Indian, and Mexican. There will be two appetizers, one main course, and two desserts from each cuisine."

"Sounds good."

He mentions that not everyone will like spicy food, so he will prepare the Thai and the Indian cuisines a little milder on the spice side.

"There will also be soups, a welcome drink, and some India and Mexican snacks to munch on until it's dinner time.

"Appetizers and these snacks are different?"

"Yes. You said the event will start at around five in the evening, and that dinner will be served around eight or so. That leaves three hours in between dancing, and talking and running around." He shrugs like it makes sense to him.

It does to me too, now that he's explained it to me.

"And on the backside of the paper you'll see a small menu for toddlers and young kids."

My gods, he's thought of everyone and everything.

"Thank you. This is perfect. I love it, and I'm sure all the attendees will too."

"I'm glad you approve of the menu."

"I approve heartily."

"Thank you."

～

AFTER WE FINISH our drinks and food, we sit in the pub for a few more minutes, then pay our bill—more like *he* pays our bill—and head out.

"What now?" I ask him.

"What do you wanna do?" Finnick asks.

"Don't you want to go back to the diner?"

"Restaurant," he corrects me, like he always does.

Finnick doesn't like calling his diner a diner. He prefers to call it restaurant. When I asked him why one day, he said diner sounds so small and insignificant. Whereas his is bigger in size and he provides a lot more at this restaurant than a diner does.

I laughed so hard at the explanation, that he spanked my ass. Literally spanked.

I know what he means, get his reason even, but it's fun to rile him.

"Fine. Don't you want to go back to your restaurant?"

"No." He shakes his head. "I hired a new head chef yesterday. He has five years of experience working as a head chef in one of the big restaurants in Los Angeles, California."

"What is he doing here leaving California?"

"What anyone does in Vale Valley."

Right.

Silly me.

"If you are free, then let's go to your place. I haven't seen your house, where you live."

"Okay. Do you want to follow me? Or join me in my car?"

"I'll follow you."

FINNICK LIVES on the hill in a modest-sized house on the outskirts of the town—well, not really, but it is far away in my opinion. Maybe not very far, but some twenty-five miles away from the downtown.

It's peaceful here, and very, very quiet.

There are a few spattering of houses in his neighborhood, but they are few and far between. However his plot size is big.

I like it.

The inside of the house is also well furnished and decorated, very masculine. You know the typical dark-colored stuff.

It definitely needs a little color. Just a smidge of it.

"I like your house, Finnick. It's very cute, but I don't like this gray shadow you have going on around it. It's too dull and dark."

"I know. At the time it suited me perfectly fine, but I'm thinking of renovating it."

"Where will you live if you renovate this house?"

"There's a separate two-room in-law suite in the backyard. I can live there temporarily when the renovation starts."

"Then definitely get this mediocre house turned into a beauty."

"I will," he says over his shoulder, as he walks toward the kitchen.

I go and perch myself on the sofa, making myself at home.

Finnick comes back with two bottles of water, two glasses, and a wine bottle.

He hands me one bottle, and I drain it immediately. He finishes his as well, then pours wine for both of us.

"Cheers." We clink our glasses, then take a sip.

"Umm, this is good. I think I have had this before at Rosemary's home."

"I like it too. I got it from 12 Grapes." He sits on the other end of the sofa.

"Oh, the winery that is run by Ty and Felix Tyche? I have heard their wines have luck-themed names. Which one is this?"

"Lucky in Love."

My mouth curves and his eyes twinkle. "Just what we need," I mutter under my breath, and he still hears. Shifter hearing. We hear everything even when we don't want to.

He takes my glass from my hand and places it on the coffee table along with his glass, then pulls me closer between his legs, my back resting against his chest. He wraps his arm over my chest and heaves a contented sigh.

The beat of his heart warbles with my heart, creating the music of love and affection.

I close my eyes and relish the feeling of oneness between us.

I've never dreamed I'd have this?

Okay, so I've dreamed about it, but never gave it a thought.

I didn't think it would ever come true this soon.

I always thought I would have time to find love and a mate after I'd established my business, and have a steady flow of income. Which has happened—and a lot sooner than I thought.

Sometimes I wonder if all this is an illusion my mind is crafting.

The fear of all of it being snatched from my grasp is my greatest worry. I have had nightmares about it on consecutive nights a short while ago.

I'm afraid of expressing this to Finnick. What if he finds it silly? I find it silly some nights, but other nights when the terror is fresh and still alive in my head, not so much.

"What are your plans for Thanksgiving?" Finnick asks, pulling my head out of my thoughts.

"Hmmm?"

"What are you doing on Thanksgiving?"

"I'll be with my family. What about you?"

"Where I come from, we don't celebrate Thanksgiving."

"Oh." Now that he's said it, I don't know where he's actually from. I don't know anything about him. "Where do you come from? How old are you?"

"Western India. I'm from western India. I'm forty one years old."

Forty one? My brows knot and I look at him. He looks like he's in his early thirties. Good genes I guess.

"Old I know." Finnick shrugs his shoulders.

"Not old, just Daddy material!" I wink.

He laughs and shakes his head, then a somber look enters his eyes. "My ma—Misha was from Turkmenistan. He was a honey badger too. We met on a cruise. I was a chef and he was the shore excursion manager. But then I got a job in a seven star hotel in South Africa and we moved there."

He becomes quiet. I cock my head to the side and look up over my shoulder. His eyes have grown distant, almost empty, and his face has that downturned look.

"I'm sorry if my questions have made you sad. That was not my intention."

"I know. I'm just sad because of the way they died. Did I tell you Misha was pregnant? I found out when I received the post-mortem report. He was only seven weeks into his pregnancy. "

"No! That's so sad." Gods, my heart aches for him. No one should have to lose their mate and kids to senseless killing. "I'm sorry." I kiss his chin.

"Me too, love."

My breath hitches and I freeze in his arms. The single

word sends a tingling thrill through my veins, shaking my heart into overdrive.

Think about something else.

"Do you want to come to my place for Thanksgiving?" I blurt the question, holding my breath.

"I don't want to impose on your family time."

"You won't. I have been wanting to invite you to come, but wasn't sure if you would like it or not."

"Are you sure? What will your parents think?"

"I have already informed them I want to invite someone special."

"Special, huh?"

"Yupp." I pull out of his arms and twist my body, then straddle him. I cup his cheeks in my hands and look into his eyes. "You are special to me, Finnick. I don't know what is going on between us, what we are, but I want more from this relationship than I have ever wanted from any other."

"We are dating is what's going on. We are lovers is what we are. And I want more too. I just don't want to rush and have any kind of regret festering between us."

"I know. And I lo—admire you for it. But we don't need to be careful. I want you. May it be for just a few more months, or forever."

"You want forever with me?" Emotions swim in his eyes, strong and shimmering.

"I do, if you can put up with my cranky hoe ass."

"I love your cranky ass." He squeezes my buns for emphasis.

"Good to know." I smirk and give him a chaste kiss on his lips. "So you'll come? For Thanksgiving lunch?"

"If you are sure about it?"

"I'm sure, so please come."

"Okay. I'll bring some desserts. Tell your mom I'm in-charge of desserts."

"Why don't you come to my house and cook. That way you can get to know my family as well. We all help cook."

"Okay, that sounds wonderful. I'll be there after breakfast."

"Okay." I also want to ask him to have breakfast with us as well, but don't want to pressure him too much. I'm just happy he's agreed to come for Thanksgiving lunch.

I hug him, then rest my head on his shoulder, and blow out a satisfied sigh.

"You smell good," Finnick murmurs in my ear. "You smell like pine and forest and sunshine."

I pull back and flick my imaginary hair like a haughty diva. "Why, thank you. It takes a lot of effort to smell this good. But I can't say the same about you."

"You..." He pushes me on my back and pounces on me like a predator, then tickles the hell out of me.

"N-no... s-s-st-a-p!" I stutter, between my laughter and gasps. "P-please..." I kick my legs, buck my hips to get him off. "... s-stop."

"Serves you right for saying I smell bad."

"I was only jesting. I didn't mean it."

"Sure you didn't" He tickles me some more, then captures my mouth, kissing me senseless. My body relaxes, and I give in to his call, surrendering to the kiss.

His teeth graze my lips, sending tingles down my spine to my toes.

My being sighs, a satisfied warmth blankets me.

I get lost in the kiss, capitulate to my desire for him. This time I will be aware of my surroundings, my emotions, my need for him. I will remember every detail of the pleasure I receive from him. Every moan, every growl coming out of his mouth feels good. It fuels my inner fervor.

His lips trail, leaving wet kisses across my jaw, my neck.

He licks a spot, his tongue rolling in a lazy circles on a patch of skin.

"You taste good too," Finnick says, nibbling the skin between the crook of my neck and shoulder.

People will now see the proof of our love making, unless I hide it.

A small part of me wants to hide and keep everything that happens between us. My selfish ass wants him all to myself.

Is that possessiveness I'm feeling?

And there's nothing wrong with feeling possessive.

He's mine, and I'll be damned if I will let anyone take him away from me.

I whimper when his hands pull my t-shirt up and glide up my torso.

He abandons my neck and focuses his attention on my nipples, kissing, licking, then sucking on them.

My entire body goes crazy when his warm breath tickles the sensitive skin around my nipples.

I buck my hips, wanting to feel him closer, feel his arousal.

He looks up, and I skim my gaze over his face.

"You brought my heart back to life."

I suck in a breath, my heart stilling from his words.

"You brought me out of the darkness." He says in a hoarse voice.

I shake my head, and stay still beneath him.

"You are what I'm thankful for this year, and for the rest of my life."

My vision blurs as tears fill my eyes. His words, they break me and build up again.

Taking a shuddering breath, I lever up on my right elbow and brush my lips against his, slowly snaking the other hand around his neck.

I move my lips over his, pressing, devouring them. He

whimpers when I sink my teeth into his swollen lower lip, his eyes closing. My tongue sweeps against his lips, probing him to open.

I buck my hips and grind against his groin. He gasps and moans, parting his lips. I plunge my tongue into his mouth, the sweet taste of wine still lingers, washing over me.

He presses his body, heat seeping into every fiber of my being. Nothing is sweet about this moment. Nothing at all. Yet it is.

It's fire.

It's raw.

It's ashes.

There's nothing washed out about what we are doing, and this is just foreplay. Just the start of pleasure. There's still the whole journey to the light at the end of the tunnel.

And I'll wish for it, reach for it, like the falling star it is.

Sui generis.

Unexampled.

Beautiful.

If a kiss like this can revive my dull soul, I wonder what his cock inside me will do.

Wonders. I'm sure it'll do wonders, and I'll finally get a chance to experience the celestial nirvana.

I'll find out soon. Maybe not today, or even tomorrow, but some day soon.

I pull back, tearing my mouth from his, ending the passionate spit swapping and filling my lungs with much-needed air.

"Need to stop," I pant.

"Yeah." He rolls off me and sits.

Suddenly a cellphone buzzes somewhere, and I realize the ringtone is mine. It sounds distant. I hurriedly get off the sofa and look around for it.

"Shit, where is my phone?"

"I think it's coming from under the sofa," Finnick says.

I bend down and look under the sofa. "It's not here."

I get up and check in the kitchen.

I may have left it there when I was touring the house with Finnick.

"Found it!" Finnick shouts.

I rush toward him. "Where was it?"

"Inside the sofa cushions. Must have gone inside when we were playing tonsils hockey."

The cellphone stops ringing, but I still check the log to see who's called me.

It's one of my flower suppliers, Jenny.

I'm about to lock my cellphone when I receive a message from her. She's asking me to meet her to finalize the flowers for the thank you event.

"I have to go. One of my flower suppliers is asking to meet to finalize my event order."

"Oh, okay." His face falls.

I'm not happy about the intrusion either, but duty calls. And when duty calls, you freaking go.

Should I ask him to come?

"Do you want to join me?" I ask.

"Sure. I have nothing better to do."

CHAPTER 11

FINNICK

It's the Thanksgiving day and I have been at Oscar's parents' place since 10 am this morning. I have enjoyed every minute of my time with them.

Meeting his family has felt like sealing the deal. Like we are finally letting the family know we are serious about each other. Which we are.

I'm very serious about him, about our relationship, about our future.

Maybe it's too soon to say, but I know I'm falling for him. And that's the thing about shifters. We fall in love fast and hard. And we mate for life as well. At least honey badgers do.

His family has been very accepting. They are a very down-to-earth kind of people. They like to crack jokes, pull each other's legs, tease and laugh.

They are one of those Hallmark Channel families. And I'm loving being part of it today.

It's a bit overwhelming, but in a good way.

I was nervous when I first arrived, but when I sat down and had a cup of tea with his mom and dad, I settled down a bit.

After that, it was smooth sailing and everything came easily. The conversation, the banter, and even the interrogation.

His father, Justin Nutter, works at the Vale Valley General Hospital in the admin department in one of the hospital buildings in the campus, and his mom, Geneva Nutter, works at the Vale Valley Pack and Snack Grocery Store.

Oscar has five siblings. The twins, Blake and Angie, are younger by nine years. They are in college and couldn't come home for the holiday. They are studying on the other side of the country. The other three, Landon, Chris, and Rhune are Oscar's quadruplets. They stay at home with Justine and Geneva, like Oscar. However, each of his siblings owns a business in Vale Valley, and are doing well for themselves. Landon is a carpenter and owns Timber Revival Carpentry in downtown. He makes beautiful furniture and does wood carving. Chris owns a salon, Coiffed Creations, and Rhune owns a printing press, Inked Pages.

All three are omegas like Oscar too.

It's been good so far. I have enjoyed their company, and all three are just like Oscar. Tall, handsome, and sweet, albeit a little talkative.

We have had a hearty lunch and enjoyed every delicacy that has been served. Oscar's mom has magic hands. Everything she has made today is delicious.

"What is this? It's so yummy," Landon inquires.

"Rice pudding. It is made of rice, and lots of condensed milk, and saffron."

"And what's this orange noodle like?" Rhune points at the dish with his fork.

"That's Foi thong. It is made by lightly showering egg yolks through a narrow funnel cone into a sugary syrup."

He takes a bite and closes his eyes. "It's good." He swallows and takes another bite. "Really good."

Rhune, Chris, and Landon were busy helping his dad put the Christmas tree up while I was making this.

I look at Oscar, who's next to me, scarfing the tea pie I brought with me this morning.

"Do you want some more?"

"I won't say no. this is good." He speaks around a mouthful.

"I'm glad you like it."

"You definitely should make this when I'm pregnant."

The table falls silent. Every eye in the room is on him. Oscar's cheeks flush immediately, and he realizes his mistake.

However, that doesn't stop my mouth from curving, for my chest to puff out with elation.

"Not that I'm pregnant. But some day I will be and I want you to make it for me. And there's no pressure for you to put a baby in me. I mean, I know we are not there yet, but I just thought you should know I would like to have this when I get pregnant. Maybe in a few years. If I'm all settled by then, and you are ready for it. I'm not sure when exactly that will be though."

I capture his mouth and stop his verbal diarrhea.

He gasps, his tense body relaxing instantly when I grab the nape of his neck.

I pull back and rest my forehead against him. "Whenever you are ready, you tell me and I'll put a baby in you. And I'll make tea pie for you as well," I whisper against his lips.

"Promise?"

The vulnerability is his eyes, the uncertainty in his voice tugs something in my heart.

"Yes, promise." I smile and brush my nose against his.

This time he captures my mouth, his lips moving, kissing with urgency and desperation.

"Get a room," someone, Chris I think, shouts and throws a napkin at us.

We pull back, a smile tugging both our lips.

"We will," Oscar shoots back, then throws the napkin back at Chris, then looks at me. "To be continued later."

"Okay."

No one and nothing can wipe this grin off my face. Not even the Prince of Darkness.

I FINALLY SAY goodbye to everyone and take my leave.

It takes us more than thirty minutes to clean and clear the table.

Geneva packs some of the leftovers for me in Tupperware containers for dinner.

Oscar follows me out and hugs me when we reach my car. "Thanks for coming. It was nice having you here with my family." He pulls back and grins at me.

"Thank you for inviting me. I enjoyed meeting and spending time with your family."

"My family loves you. You won them over with your cooking skills. Mom and Dad couldn't stop gushing about you."

"I'm glad they enjoyed the dessert I made."

"You can come and charm them anytime one of us is on their shit list."

I laugh and lean forward, and whisper in his ear, "Just let me know when you are in the dog house and I'll whip something up for them."

"I knew there was a reason why Fate brought us together."

"To rescue you?"

"Yes! My personal protector."

"Thank you for the title and the job I didn't ask for."

"You are welcome."

I roll my eyes, but the grin doesn't drop.

"Do you wanna come home with me?"

"Sure. I want to talk to you about something as well."

"Will you stay the night…" I jerk my chin at the house behind him. "…or come back home?"

"I want to stay the entire weekend with you. Is that okay?" His forehead wrinkles, and he bites the inside of his cheek, hands fidgeting, twisting together in front of him.

"It's more than okay."

"Thank you." His lips tip up, pearly teeth come in to nibble on my lower lips, kissing me innocently. "Give me five minutes to pack some of my stuff," he says against my lips.

"Okay. You can take more than five minutes. After all, divas need more stuff to carry with them than it is necessary."

He smacks my arm before spinning on his heel and running back inside the house.

WE ARE at my home and I have put Oscar's bag in my bedroom.

I need to make some space for his stuff in my closet, so he can keep a few items and some clothes here for when he stays the night.

The idea of having him in my space sends a thrill to my soul. My heart likes the idea of having him and his scent in the house.

We are sitting on the porch and having a glass of wine. "So what did you want to talk about?"

"Well…" he pushes the hair out of his face and swallows. "I

want to ask... that is… I wanted to know what you... think—if you are okay with it… that is, if you don't mind..."

"I won't mind, now tell me what has you so nervous."

He jumps out of his chair and paces the length of my back porch. "My heat is coming," he blurts out, stopping in front of me. He grimaces and shakes his head slightly.

"Okay."

Does he not want my help? Is that what this is about?

Even though he hasn't said exactly those words, I feel that's where he is heading.

And that thought stings more than I thought it ever would.

"I want you to help me with my heat."

Oh.

Oh!

He wants my help.

A profound relief and excitement accelerates through my veins, leaving me lightheaded.

I blink a few times and crush the grin wanting to curve my mouth.

Act nonchalant.

Don't show your eagerness.

"Okay, I'll help you. When's your heat coming?"

"Should be this Saturday, or Sunday."

"You don't know?"

"It's Saturday, but sometimes, due to stress it delays for a few hours."

"Got it. How long are your heats usually?"

"Two to three days. Unless..." he bites his lips, frowning.

"Unless?"

"Unless I'm trying to get pregnant. In that case, the heat will vanish as soon as I conceive. So, it can be a day, or just a few hours. Depends how much time it takes to lock up the baby makers."

"Hmmm." I stare at nothing for an overlong moment, but snap back when Oscar nudges me with his foot.

"What are you thinking?"

"If I should wear a condom or not."

"Oh."

"Do you want me to? Cover my junk, I mean?"

"Answer a question for me first."

"Okay?"

"How serious are we? Where do you see this relationship going?"

"I'm very serious about us, and I'm all in."

"Okay." He nods, and repeats again, "Okay."

"I'm falling for you. Fast and hard. Didn't see it coming, but it's happening. And I do not want to back away. What about you? Where do you stand in this relationship?"

"I love you!" he blurts out.

My breath catches in my chest, and I sit stunned for several beats.

Everything has short-circuited inside me.

My whole nervous system is doing one-eighty cartwheels in every direction.

"I'm happy to know."

Really, Finnick? You are happy to know?

Ugh. That's not what I wanted to say.

I get up and it's me who's pacing this time.

Like I said, nothing is in sync.

My brain is thinking one thing, but my mouth is saying something else.

I stop a short distance from him and face him. "What I mean is, me too."

Ugh. *Get a grip, asshole!*

I slap my right cheek and slightly shake my head and body.

As if that'll right my crazy, wires-crossed brain.

Still it's worth a try. Anything to get my head straightened and thinking and saying the correct stuff.

I take a deep breath and meet his wary gaze.

"I love you too. I know it's way too soon to say and feel like this, but that's how I feel for you."

"How do you feel?"

"Like I cannot breathe without talking to you for even a day. Like the sun is dull and meaningless without seeing your face. Like the breath in my body is meant for only you. I cannot sleep without dreaming of you. I cannot do anything without thinking about you. Your smile lights up my day, your laughter brightens my mood. You, your presence brings me back to life!"

Tears are spilling down Oscar's cheeks, his face is beet red, shining, his body trembling.

There's no caution, no hesitation, nor there is any doubt in his eyes or on his face.

He believes every word that has come out of my mouth. Every single word. Which elates my already-happy heart, lifting my mending spirit.

Oscar stamps out the distance between us in a few strides and winds his arms around me in a painful grip, hugging me, kissing my cheeks, my jaw, each and every surface on my face.

"I love you too." He caresses my lips with his. "I love you so much. I feel exactly like how you feel. I miss you at night, wishing you were with me. My day feels hollowed out when I don't hear your voice. You mean *everything* to me. Life is boring without your grumpiness, Mr. Grooch."

"If you say so, Mr. Sunshine."

"So, no protection during my heat?"

"Only if you'll mate with me."

"When?"

That's all he wants to know, and that makes me even happier.

"You don't want a ceremony and invite your family?"

"Nope. My parents are not into traditions. If we say want the mating to happen without an audience, my parents will support us."

"Still I want to ask their permission before claiming you."

"We can do that tomorrow."

"Sounds good."

CHAPTER 12

OSCAR

With a groan, I wake up, feeling hot and bothered. Every muscle in my body aches,.

I feel feverish, my insides burning.

I look for my water bottle and find it's not there.

Hmm, strange.

The smell in the room is strange.

Whose room is this?

I look around and realize I've been staying at Finnick's place since Thursday night.

What day is today?

I check the digital clock on the side table.

3 a.m., Saturday.

The fuck am I doing being awake at the asscrack of dawn?

I roll my neck, a prickling feeling slithers down my back.

Finnick turns and wraps his arm over my chest.

Inadvertently, I lean toward him and sniff his scent.

The whiff of his smell fills my nostrils, blending into my bloodstream, sending tingles into my veins. I whimper and get closer to him.

My spirit shivers, trembling with need.

Aimlessly, my left leg lifts and rolls over him, my arousal rubbing against his sleeping shaft.

Finnick groans, his arm pulling me closer.

The feel of his body heat charging against mine... caressing, kissing. I feel lightheaded.

Altered.

Breathless.

I push him onto his back and straddle him.

Unable to stop myself, I grind over his slowly waking dick.

I bite the inside of my cheek, and wonder when I turned into such a horny hoe.

Then a thought punches me in the ass.

I'm in heat.

Excitement and fear, both curl into the pit of my stomach, sending a rush of blood to my cock.

An airless whimper floats out of my lips, my chest rising faster with breathlessness.

I lean down and flick my tongue over his right nipple, drawing a sleepy moan from Finnick's lips.

Not enough.

A feeling of emptiness still sits at the bottom of my stomach..

Want more.

Need more.

I get off him and remove my pajama pants and t-shirt, then slowly untie Finnick's pants strings.

He startles awake, eyes large, frantically looking around.

"I'm in heat." I say and pull his pants down.

"What?"

"I'm in heat."

"Oh."

He scrambles off the bed and quickly shucks the remaining fabric on his body.

Beads of sweat coat the back of my neck, trickling down my spine.

Suddenly my ass clenches, and slick leaks out of my hole.

I moan and lean forward, a dizzy spell shaking me.

"Finnick," I call him desperately, slick running down between my legs. "Need you. P-please..."

"I'm here, love." He pulls me into his arms, and kisses my lips. "Come, sweet. I'll take care of you."

Thank gods!

Finnick stacks a few pillows and leans on his back and motions for me to get on top of him. "Ride me."

I don't waste any time. I don't have enough time to waste with slick gushing out of my ass.

I climb over him and roughly guide him inside me, and I cry out in relief, my whole body shaking, feeling full.

A growl reverberates at the back of Finnick's throat, and it sends a sweet thrill through my heated veins.

He grabs my hips and guides me up and down his length, setting a pace.

I roll my hips, and swallow him whole inside me.

Finnick leans forward and suckles on my sensitive nipples.

Suck, bite, lap.

I slam down on him, an outpouring of pleasure into every tendril of my soul.

I pant, he grunts, flames shoot inside me, a building up of nirvana consuming me.

Bit by bit.

Breath by breath.

Suck, bite, lap.

The trend follows, until I'm a mess of feelings.

I feel too much. Inside and out.

My breath comes out shorter and shorter, hot air blending between us.

I swallow his breath.

He swallows mine.

Sweat dribbles down our chests, the room smelling of sex and arousal. He grabs my arms and tugs them behind my back, then his fingers glide down my spine.

"Keep your hands behind you. Don't move them at all. And just feel, Oscar."

I blow out a shuddering breath, my body begging, crying for comfort.

He pulls my bottom lips between his teeth, suckling on it. His lips trail, kissing my jaw, then biting the shell of my ear.

"Feel everything. Enjoy your heat, you hear me. Enjoy it, because I will."

I whimper when he licks the length of my neck, tasting my sweat.

I moan and rut against him, seeking attrition, seeking the light I know is there for me.

Catch it.

Grab it.

My hips move faster, and harder.

He grazes his fingers over the length of my dick, and rubs the sticky liquid coming from the slit all over my cock, then circles his fingers around the girth of my twitching shaft.

Up and down, those fingers move, and a pinprick of tantalizing awareness builds at the base of my spine, opening out, stretching into my reality.

Bending his head, his lips capture the soft skin on my chest, and mark it with his teeth.

"Finnick..." I sob, my heart racing, my pulse lashing out.

He lifts his head, his eyes burning molten fire. Unwrapping his fingers, he guides them to my back, and his palms hold my shoulders in a brutal grip.

And then he's lifting us into the air.

I squeal, my hands abandon their position and latch on to his hair. He grunts and then I'm on my back. I lose my breath, my heart full, eyes fluttering.

I look into his eyes, his gaze rolling across my lips.

"You are beautiful, you know?" His coarse voice opens something inside me. Even my heat-addled mind knows this is something special and I should savor it.

"Love me, Finnick." I clench my ass around his shaft. "Make me yours."

His lips tug up into that cocky smile I get to see very rarely on his handsome face, his eyes pinning me with such fierceness. "With pleasure!"

And he thrusts into me, filling me to the hilt.

My mouth opens and I gasp as he pumps into me faster and harder, stretching me, filling me, lighting my soul with fireworks.

He captures my mouth, kissing me with so much feeling, and hammers into me, faster and faster, sending my heart and breath scattering.

I inhale his grunts, his shuddering heaves. My fingers sink into his shoulders, legs snake around his hips, pulling him closer to me.

We beat as one.

Breathe as one.

Our souls weave, becoming one Ka as the Egyptians like to call it.

Our pleasure and passion become the epitome of firelight.

Burning.

Intense.

Consuming.

Total bliss.

A shooting star meant to shine and blaze like the sun.

Our bodies move.

Thrust to thrust.

Pants and gasp.

Pelvis bucking, cock twitching.

I scream and arch my back as his teeth nip my bottom lip. A whimper molds in the back of my throat, and I graze his back with my nails.

A smell of copper charges through the air and Finnick grunts. "Harder," he grates, pulling back.

I look into his eyes.

"Mark me harder, love!"

I dig my nails deeper, tearing his skin. I lean forward and sink my teeth into his shoulder.

He whimper groans, his cock twitching inside me, then his pace increases, his balls slapping against my ass, echoing between the walls.

He grabs the nape of my neck and tugs my face closer, kissing me into oblivion.

He pushes and pushes me, bringing me to the fringe of the tunnel, toward the ecstasy, heating me inside-out.

Heart thundering, release edging, I climb the peak. High, high, I go up. My body arches into him, feels the shaking of his body.

He clenches his jaw, eyes frantic, rear moving at a frenzied pace.

I'm on the edge of the cliff with him.

Just us.

"I'm close. Very close…"

He enters with a mighty push, his knot swelling at the base of his dick.

I whimper as his knot fills my ass, stretching beyond capacity.

His thrusts become smaller, shallower, yet he manages to hit the sweet spot in my ass.

Afresh.

Anew every time.

I scream out a name, his name rolling on my tongue, and his release sears into me.

Arising up like a celestial entity.

A gift for eternity fusing into the Milky Way.

Light flashes behind my eyes, and our bodies are a blend of liquid molten lava.

Scorching.

Sizzling.

We have created an inferno, our pleasure a firestorm, surrounding us like a cloak of chaos.

Magic.

Him and me.

An illusion of the future.

Us.

A unity.

I explode, and he stills inside me. Our orgasms ripping through our bodies.

I shudder and writhe under him, his limbs tremble with the effort of keeping going.

A deep moan belts out of my mouth, our gazes lock, my being coming alive from the scrutiny.

I clench my ass, sucking his cock tight.

His lips part and he leans forward, and sinks his teeth into the crook of my shoulder, just behind my neck and claims me, sending my blood pounding into my head, its rush buzzing in my ear, wave after wave.

My body rocks. I feel my heart coming out, howling.

Claim him!

Become his!

I open my mouth and pierce my teeth into his warm, sweaty flesh, drawing blood and a guttural groan from him. He gyrates his hips, more of his seed filling my channel.

His knot is at its full size in my ass.

I moan and writhe, my whimpers floating through the air.

Tremor after tremor rakes my body, and I clutch his arousal like it's my lifeline.

Like he's my faith.

Our souls knit together, binding us for life.

Until death do us part.

THE SECOND SURGE arrives sooner than we anticipate, and it is just as wild as the first one.

We are in the shower where Finnick takes me against the wall.

Rough and raw.

Wild and crazy.

And I am loving every moment of it.

FOR THE THIRD SURGE, Finnick takes me doggy style, pounding my ass from behind.

He is fierce in giving me pleasure.

He has broken me apart so many times today, I have lost count.

And has broken me in a good way.

He rocks my world.

And now that I'm sated and fulfilled, I lie awake, curled in Finnick's arms. Finnick is snoring behind me, his warm breath caressing my cold skin.

I listen to the rhythmic beat of his heart thrumming against my back, his pulse a steady clock for my heart.

I smooth a kiss gently on his hand that is resting across my chest.

I loose a contented sigh, and close my eyes.

"You awake?" Finnick croaks from behind me.

"Yeah."

"Not getting any sleep?"

"No." I shake my head slightly.

"Something bothering you?" He spoons me, tightening is ams around me.

"Nothing. I'm just so happy. Content."

"Hmmm." He press a gentle kiss on my shoulder. "You are my mate now. My omega!"

Excitement bounces through me at his words, sending a thrill to my heart.

"I am. And you are my Alpha."

"My mate."

"My mate."

His fingers run a lazy circle over my heart and slide down over to my stomach, splaying them across it.

"You might be with a child."

"Or children."

"My gods, I'll be a blessed man if it's more than one," his voice turns hoarse. "I'll be a blessed man if the gods will bestow us with anything." He laughs, his chest vibrating against my back. "Who am I kidding, I'm already a blessed man. I have you, my mate, a good, decent life, and a few babies on the way."

"Yeah, life can't get any better than this," I agree with him.

"When do you think you'll know if you are pregnant?" He plucks my earlobe between his teeth, nibbling on the rim, teasing me.

"We need to wait at least a w-week to confirm," I pant, feeling breathless and charged.

"Life is good." His lips curve into a smile against my neck. "Really good."

Yeah, it is.

But as I look into the darkness outside the window, a feeling of pinpricking needles dancing in the pit of my stomach hovers.

I can't explain it, or where it is coming from.

It's just a feeling.

A feel that has taken root and is warning me that something is hiding in the shadows, lurking, waiting to rip everything from our grasp.

CHAPTER 13

OSCAR

I can't believe I'm mated to Finnick.

Not only does the man love me, he worships me as well, and I him.

And I have realized that when Finnick loves, he loves hard. It's all consuming, and I love it.

We have been mated for a week now, and I still haven't moved all my stuff. We have decided to renovate the house and expand it.

It's all right for two people, but too small if we want to expand the family. Which we are. I'll know tomorrow if I'm pregnant with our babies.

Squirrel shifters tend to give birth to multiple babies, that is, any number between two and nine, and our gestation period ranges between four to five months.

Nine babies would definitely tear my ass. And I quite like my ass as it is.

Hopefully, I'm carrying twins or triplets.

Unfortunately, I'm not sure how my pregnancy will be, since I'm mated to a honey badger.

I'll find out tomorrow.

If I'm having multiple babies, then we will definitely need a bigger house, and this house just won't cut it out for our growing family.

We have already moved out of the house and are living in the in-law suite in the backyard, and we have dumped all the furniture and other stuff from the house into the garage.

Thank gods, Finnick has hired Wolfe Constructions to make that happen. I have heard Quintus Wolfe is amazing to work with. And his younger sisters, Miya and Ariana, who own Wolfe Interior Designers—which is a Wolfe Construction subsidiary—are helping us with the house.

I'm excited to see how everything will look after it's done.

It's hard to believe this is my new reality.

We, Finnick and I, have decided to give a small return gift to every residents who will attend the thank-you party. Plus, a surprise special thank-you gift will go to Rosemary who brought us together. If it wasn't for her suggestion, I don't think Finnick and I would have ever crossed paths in this lifetime.

Scratch that.

No, we would have crossed paths. Maybe in a few years, but we definitely would have. We are fated to meet in this life.

He is my Fated mate.

My soulmate.

I didn't realize it, but during my heat cycle, a bond has weaved, even before Finnick claiming me. It was so strong, I've seen stars.

I touch the claim mark on the back of my neck, just over my shoulder, and sigh.

Every time I touch it, a glow-like sensation tingles through me, and my heart jumps with happiness.

I'm happy. I'm beyond happy. I'm ecstatic.

Every morning and night I thank all the gods for bringing him to me.

He completes me in a way I didn't know I needed.

He's my soul.

My shooting star.

My reality.

He's my infinite abyss of happiness.

I'll cherish and savor every second of my life with him. And I will show him just how much he means to me as well.

He doesn't know it yet, but during the thank-you party, I'm going to ask Rosemary to officiate us in front of the whole town. I want the whole world to know he's mine, and I am his.

And for that I need to buy a ring for both of us. I know what his size is, and I just need to finalize on the design I want for him.

Finnick doesn't like flashy stuff, and neither do I, so I'm going to look for something that is simple and beautiful.

I browse through the internet and finally find one I like, one that is simple and beautiful. It's perfect for Finnick. A white-gold wedding ring that has three tiny diamonds at the top and three tiny diamonds to both sides.

I select something similar for myself as well.

I just need to figure out what inscription I want on the inside of the rings.

I think on it for sometime.

Do I want something sentimental and lovey dovey? Or do I want something funny and cheeky?

My heart and head latches on to funny and cheeky.

Funny and cheeky it is!

I know just the words I want on the rings. The words come naturally, and I type what I want engraved on our wedding bands. I write *'your ass is mine'* on my wedding ring, and *'paddle away my diva ass'* on his wedding ring.

Once I hit the order button, I laugh loudly.

Oh, it'll be hilarious to witness when he reads those words.

He's definitely going to grumble about it, but nothing can be done then.

The doorbell rings, and I check the time.

It's only 5 p.m., so it can't be Finnick who's ringing the doorbell.

The doorbell rings again, and again, and again, until I open the door slightly and greet a new face.

He's definitely not a part of the construction crew. I don't see the company logo, or the construction hat and high-via vest the crew usually wear.

My eyes roll down his body, checking him out. Not the I-admire-him kind of way, but like just checking him out.

He has blond hair, dark obsidian eyes, a crooked nose. There's a huge scar on his face that starts at his right eyebrow and goes down to his jaw as my focus moves to it.

He's as tall as me, and he's wearing blue faded jeans, blue and white flannel shirt, a black jacket, beanie, and boots.

Who is this man?

"Hello. How can I help you?"

"I'm looking for Finnick?"

"He'll be at the restaurant."

"Oh. And you are?" He spits the question as if it's taste is sour and he's ready to up-chuck.

Whatever asshole. I raise my china and answer him, "His mate."

His eyes darken more, and his nostrils flare. "His mate?" He grits the word out.

"Yeah."

"When did this happen?" He grinds his jaw hard, taking a step forward, and his hands clench into fists at his sides.

He raises all my hackles, and I clutch the door handle a little harder, keeping my eyes on him. "Just a few days back."

I hide my body behind the door, wishing I had my cellphone with me. But it's charging and without power it's useless to me right now.

This man is giving me creeps right now, and the urge to shut the door in his face is getting stronger and stronger by the second in his presence.

His mouth twists, an ugly sneer flashing across his face.

A seed of trepidation stampedes up my spine, nausea thumping, smacking against my belly.

Hatred burns in his eyes, strong and sinister, and I feel its punch to my heart.

His hostility is potent enough to cut the air into nothing.

The tingle in my spine intensifies, hairs at the nape of my neck rise, pulse scattering in panic.

I should send him packing.

Close the door.

Block him out.

"I think you should leave, Mister." I want to pat myself for talking so calmly, for not showing the dread I'm fighting inside me.

Do it.

Do it.

Do it.

I got to close the door, but he stops it by inserting his foot. "I don't think so," he sneers, and a vile spit sloshes out of his mouth, landing on my chin.

A prickle of alarm creeps through me, and I stand still. My heart thundering inside my chest, the seed of dread sharpening.

Crackling.

Unfurling.

Every fiber of my being screams at me to run.

Run.

Run.

Run.

With lightning fast speed, he thrusts the door open, sending me stumbling, landing on my ass.

I land awkwardly, my right elbow making contact with the floor. I cry and wince as the painful jolt buzzes through my arm. Tears fill my eyes, and fear spreads through my blood vessels.

A tip-off.

A notice.

A hint to run, to get away from him.

Before I can scream, or make sense of why this is happening to me, the man grabs my hair in a painful grip and smashes it against the floor.

I feel it before I hear the crunch of bone breaking.

Stars explode behind my eyes, and I try to grab his hand, to pull it away, but my efforts are useless against his brutal assault.

I hear the click of the door, and I know my fate has been sealed, but that doesn't stop me from hoping, from fighting.

I heave myself on my hands and knees, but I'm knocked down as the heel of his boot connects with my spine.

Pain snatches down my back, shooting a tremor through my body.

My eyes flutter closed, and tears well behind my eyelids.

Fight!

Fight!

I twist around and kick blindly, a weak effort, which enrages him.

He smacks cross my face, and pain explodes, glazing my vision.

He pulls my hair and smashes my head once more to the

floor. Then one more time. Then another, until dark spots appear in my line of sight.

He pulls his hand back and I curl into myself, my arms instinctively wrapping around my belly.

I feel numb, and my chest aches with unmeasurable horror, incapable of filling air into my lungs.

Why? Why is he hitting me?

What have I done to him?

Tears blur my eyes, and I hold in the sobs trying to come out and show how undone I am. Coiling my body tight, already knowing the onslaught of his assault is coming my way.

His vehemence pours into his fists, kicks, and words.

Breaking my spirit.

Splitting my soul.

A punishment for stealing something precious from him.

"He's mine. Always meant to be. First my brother took him, and now you want him. Never!" He kicks me hard on the hips. "I removed him, and I'll remove you as well."

Every word spilling out of his mouth is like venom.

Burning, destroying me cell by cell, inch by inch. He'll splinter me apart like I mean nothing but a roach under his sole.

"S-stop," I wheeze, my pants ragged, my lungs shrinking from the effort. "P-please stop."

"I'll never stop. Never." His leg connects to my upper back, the heel of his boots cracking something, knocking the air out of my chest.

I whimper, a shudder ripping through me.

The fear for the babies I may be carrying burns in the back of my throat, it slashes and thrashes, urging me to protect.

Save the babies!

Save the babies!

The words are screamed on repeat inside my head.

"He's mine!" The man screams and lifts his legs to kick my belly this time.

Twisting my body, I crawl, or try to. My body feels heavy, numb, loaded with the burden to survive and keep my little ones safe.

His leg connects with my side, and paint flashes through me, tearing me inside out.

I scream, my heart thundering with agony.

Go!

I try, and try and try. Move my body, push it, one inch at a time.

A guttural pained groan spills from my mouth as my body moves to that small space. I pant and clench my jaw, fight the darkness that wants to claim me, wants me to submit.

I grit my teeth and press another inch forward. The effort makes my whole body tremble.

I can't do it.

I can't do it.

The agony is too much to bear, too much to propel through.

Tears spilling, chest burning, I lie still on the floor, my arms still covering my stomach in a protective manner.

Nothing can fade this pain, nothing can trump it.

Come to me. Give in. Darkness calls.

I should give in. I should surrender. Let the darkness pull me into its pit.

Give in. Give in. Give in.

I will. I am.

Somewhere the noise of a door opening blares through the haze of pain, and I hear Finnick's voice.

Clenching my teeth, I lift my face—barely—off the floor and look around.

I scent him before I see him.

It is Finnick.

Our gaze meets, his eyes filled with horror and rage.

I open my mouth, but gasp when I see a knife in the man's hands.

"Run," I whisper, and close my eyes as unconsciousness knocks me into oblivion.

CHAPTER 14

FINNICK

The trickle of unease has been growing in the pit of my stomach since this afternoon. I don't know why, but I'm not ignoring it.

It's the same feeling I had years ago when my cete was attacked by feral hyenas.

But today it has been intensifying with each passing second.

I should call home and check on him.

I speed dial his number and it goes straight to voicemail. I call him again. Same thing happens.

I send him a message. I don't see the delivered report at the bottom of the message.

Should I call Quintus on his cellphone and ask him to check on Oscar?

I don't want to seem too hovering and paranoid, but the feeling is just escalating.

Grabbing my keys from my office, I start walking out of the restaurant, not bothering to remove my apron and chef's whites.

I press the fob and unlock the car and sit behind the wheel, nerves racing,

I reach home in record time, and park the car outside the garage, then jog toward the in-law suite in the backyard.

A scream splinters through the air as I near the suite, and dread spirals in my chest, twisting into a big knot, blocking the air from entering my chest.

I stand rooted, my legs locked firmly to the ground.

Another scream.

My heart sinks, pulse thrashes against my veins.

Oscar!

I blink several times, trying to banish the haze, but the past comes barreling back, and all I see is blood, gore, people from my cete screaming and keening, fighting for their lives.

Rohan's lifeless frame.

Misha's torn body.

Mom and Dad ripped to shreds.

"Finnick, what was that noise?" Quintus Wolfe asks me. "Was that a scream?"

My head turns toward him, and dazed, I look at him.

"Was that Oscar's scream?" I blink a few more times, unable to form words. He grabs my shoulder and shakes me. "Finnick, man, are you okay? I'm calling Sheriff LeMarkus Vale."

Another scream reverberates from the suite.

My heart slams against my chest, pulse lashing out.

Go, save him!

The sinister growl coming from inside the house breaks the spell the past has been having on me, and my legs finally move.

He needs you! Misha's words bounce in my head.

My body propels forward, my brain screaming at me to hurry up, to work faster.

Stumbling, tripping on my legs, I make it to the door.

With trembling hand, I twist the door knob, and find it locked,

My shaky fingers remove the house key from my pants pocket. The attempt to insert the key into the lever takes a few tries.

When it finally latches into the combination disc, I twist the knob and open the door.

The scene that I come face-to-face to with the one I will never ever forget in my life. It's the scene from a horror movie.

It's the scene my nightmares will play on repeat from here onward.

Dimitri is holding a knife in his hands about to plunge it into Oscar, who's lying on the floor, bloody and shaking.

"D-dimitri? What are you doing here?"

"What you shouldn't have done!" he screams, a look of madman on his face.

"What are you talking about?" Fear slices through me, my eyes constantly jump between him and Oscar.

My chest tightens watching my mate lying on the floor like this. My eyes take in every detail. Blood-smeared face, swollen nose, split lips, arms covering his stomach, knees blocking the view and access to his belly.

Is he pregnant? We were supposed to find out tomorrow if we are.

But the way he's protecting his... My heart thrashes when I realize that he must be. He must be with a child or two.

My gaze jumps back on Dimitri.

Why is Dimitri here?

Why are you doing this?

"You were supposed to see me after Misha was gone, but you always looked past me. Like I didn't exist. You were supposed to *see* me, take notice of me."

Oh, gods, this can't be happening!

"Dimitri, come on, man. You are my family."

"No, no. No!" He whirls in my direction, rage and contempt flashing in his gaze, and points the knife at me. "I don't want to be *that* kind of family. I want to be your mate. You hear me, *your mate!* But you always choose someone lesser than me. Always." He looks down at Oscar like he's another bug that needs to be squashed. "I will kill him too, just like I erased our family who came between me and you."

Shock ricochets through me, disgust barbs through my being. "You killed our family?" I take in a shuddering breath. "You killed your brother and nephew?"

I fist my hands at my sides, my insides twisting with disbelief.

How could he do that?

How could he murder his own brother and nephew, his blood?

Why haven't I seen this side of him?

This is all my fault.

My fault.

When I claimed Misha, I took pity on Dimitri and made him quit his job to join us in South Africa.

I should have known something was wrong with him, the way Misha avoided being in his presence.

I chalked it up as Misha being annoyed with his little brother.

But now I know why Misha didn't like having Dimitri in our house.

"I did," he smirks, one side of his lips tipping up into a sinister smile. "You are mine. *Mine!*" He screams like the devil he is. "I'm done being on the sideline. I gave you time to grieve, to move on, but you chose this piece of shit instead!" He kicks Oscar in his side, drawing a whimper out of him.

Fury laces through my already-hot burning blood, rising up, up, up. My vision turns red, and my sanity dematerializes, and I charge forward with a growl, and ram into him with my shoulder.

We both stumble on the coffee table. I pull back, my face twisting with rage.

Dimitri's eyes widen, shock blinking on his face.

Grabbing his jacket collar, I pull him up and punch him in the face, then kick him between his legs.

He grunts and falls down to his knees, eyes welling, face contorting in agony.

He doubles over in pain, groaning, moaning.

I lean down to try to grapple the knife out of his hands, but he wraps his leg around my ankles. I twist my upper body to get out of his hold, to free at least my right leg out of the lock, but he suddenly bends his knees and kicks behind my left knee. Loosing my balance, I fall down on my sides.

The fall knocks the wind out of me, and I grunt from the impact. Pain penetrates through my left shoulder.

Fuck!

That hurt.

Quickly, I scramble to my knees and crawl over to him, and plant my knee on his groin, pressing down with all my strength. I try again to wrestle the knife out of his hand, before he decides to pierce it into Oscar's chest, but even with the pressure on his crotch, he doesn't loosen his hold.

I will *not* lose my mate again.

I will *not* allow Dimitri to take him as well.

Never again.

Hatred burns for him, the man who is supposed to be my family, but has turned into a psychopathic murderer. My roiling emotions come unhinged, and the disgust I feel for him unleashes.

With a growl I pin his hands on either side of him and lean down and rip his left ear off with my bare teeth.

He screams and thrashes his head from side to side, eyes wide and wild.

I spit it out, then use my shoulder to wipe the blood off my mouth.

"You ripped my ear!" He mewls.

"I should do more than just ripping your ear," I spit, then punch him once more.

I turn around when I hear footsteps pounding into the room.

Sheriff LeMarkus Vale, Rosemary, Chance Knight, and Quintus barrel into the tiny house.

I heave a sigh of relief, my heart finally slowing down.

"Finnick!" Quintus shouts, his eyes widening, finger pointing toward Dimitri.

My head snaps in his direction, eyes falling on the knife pointed at my heart.

"If I can't have you no one will," Dimitri snarls, the tip of the knife piercing through my skin.

The sting is sharp and spiky.

My eyes widen in horror, breath lodging in my throat, my heart hammering against my chest wall.

Desolation takes over, drowning me with regret and lost opportunity.

My gaze revet back to my unconscious mate.

I'm sorry.

This is not how things are supposed to go.

Just then a shot rings through the air, and warm liquid splashes across my face.

My body stills, everything inside me stills. Pressure builds behind my eyes, dark spots invade my sight.

My eyes roll back, and everything disappears.

⁓

THE WOUND on my chest is shallow. It doesn't need any stitches, and all the nurse has done is slap on two butterfly bandages.

Other than that, I don't have any other bruises on me, except for my swollen knuckles and bruised shoulder. They'll heal in a few days.

Unfortunately, Oscar hasn't been that lucky. He's still unconscious, hooked to various machines in the hospital.

I'm sitting next to him, holding his hand.

He has multiple fractures in various places, busted lips, concussion, a fracture to his skull.

He'll be very disappointed and angry that he cannot attend the thank-you party he's hosting.

Rosemary has promised to gather a few volunteers to help her with the preparations.

And I'm thankful for that.

We still don't know if he's pregnant or not. Still waiting for the bloodwork results.

"Hey." Landon enters the room. "I'm free today. Why don't I sit with him for a while and give you a little time to get freshened up?" He looks pointedly at the dried blood in my hair.

I washed as best as I could after waking up in the hospital.

The nurses had cleaned my face of the blood, but not my neck and head.

"Are you sure?"

"Yeah. And why don't you grab something to eat as well?"

"Okay. I'll see you in an hour. Don't leave him alone."

"I won't, Finnick. Promise." He makes a cross sign on his heart.

I nod and head out.

～

OSCAR IS ALREADY UP JUST as I enter his room in the hospital.

"Hey." I quickly take a seat next to him. "How are you feeling?"

"Drugged."

"Good stuff." I pat his hand. "You'll feel better soon."

"I want to shift, but not sure if the drugs will block my ability to do that."

"They shouldn't. And how about you wait for a few hours before shifting? Your external wounds are healing."

"Pros to being a shifter." He shrugs his shoulders, but winces, his face contorting from the agony. "But I'll heal more quickly if I shift."

"I know."

"Everything hurts. Every muscle and bone. I don't want to miss the party I'm hosting. I want to attend, be there with everyone else," he chokes, his lips wobbling.

I put my hand on top of his and squeeze it. "Let's see how you are feeling after a few days, then we'll decide, okay?"

"Okay," Oscar answers, somewhat mollified.

We sit in silence for a while. I'm just thankful Oscar is still in my life. that I didn't lose him.

But I almost came close to losing him. Very close.

"Who was that man?" Oscars question snaps my brain, forcing it to abandon the thoughts churning inside it.

"My brother-in-law. Misha's… baby brother."

"He's in love with you. Borderline obsessive kind of love."

"Was, my love. He was in love. He's dead."

"W-what? You?" His eyes grow large, lips wobbling.

I shake my head. "Nope. I didn't get that pleasure."

"How?" He blinks.

And so I tell him, spilling the event's details, explaining how I arrived, about our scuffle, his confession to killing my family and cete members.

"LeMarkus shot him when Dimitri tried to kill me."

"So he won't come back?"

"No, he won't."

"And the b-babies?" His voice breaks, fear sloshing in his eyes.

"We should know in a bit."

I'm scared of the results. I don't want to hear bad news after everything we've been through today.

The doctor arrives an hour later with Oscar's blood results. "Congratulations, you are pregnant!" The doctor smiles.

Warmth radiates throughout my body, my heart racing, drumming in my chest.

I look to Oscar and find him crying silently.

"I was so afraid I hadn't protected my baby well enough."

"Everything is fine. You need to start taking prenatal vitamins, drink plenty of water, eat healthy food, and get some good exercise.

"Exercise?" Oscar moans, and I laugh.

"Walking, light jogging should help."

"Okay," he agrees reluctantly.

"An ultrasound nurse technician will come and do a quick ultrasound for you guys in a moment."

"Thank you."

"Book your next appointment before you leave today."

"We'll do it."

"Take care, you both." With that the doctor is out of the room.

"We are having a baby!" he squeals, then hisses in pain.

"Easy there." I kiss his temple.

"I love you." He leans into me.

"I love you too."

EPILOGUE 1

FINNICK

The thank-you party has been a success. Everyone has enjoyed it. People have danced, laughed and eaten the food.

To say Oscar is happy, is an understatement.

The best surprise of the night has been claiming Oscar in front of our gathered guests. Rosemary officiated for us, and Landon and Chris stood up as our witnesses.

I look at the wedding band on my finger and can't help but laugh.

Paddle away my diva ass.

Only Oscar could think of coming up with something funny and cheeky for the inscriptions to engrave inside our rings.

My eyes search for him, darting from face to face around the hall. I find him sitting closer to the food stall.

I push through the crowd, shoving a few, greeting plenty, accepting congratulations and pats on my shoulders.

I reach Oscar after what feels like an eternity.

"Hey." I take the empty seat next to him. "How are you feeling?"

"Stop hovering and worrying so much. I'm fine."

"And the babies?"

"They are fine too."

We found out yesterday that Oscar is carrying triplets.

The first ultrasound didn't show anything properly, because it was way too early in the pregnancy. We decided to wait for a few more days and come back again, which was yesterday.

Oscar is happy, so I'm happy too.

We'll know what he's carrying when he enters the third month into his pregnancy.

"I'm hungry," he announces.

"What do you want?"

"Some dessert and Indian appetizers."

"Coming right up."

I quickly fill a plate for him and myself. His with appetizers and desserts, mine with the main course.

"Here you go." I put his plate in front of him, and mine next to him.

I go get us both a glass of fresh juice as well.

He scarfs his food down in less than five minutes, then sips the juice.

"How long do we have to stay? My head is aching."

"It's your party, but if you want to leave now we can do it. The guests will understand if you are not feeling good."

"So, we can leave?"

"Sure. I'll let your family and Rosemary know."

I gobble my food as fast I can, then go looking for Oscar's family—my family.

I find his parents and siblings standing in a corner, talking with a few residents of Vale Valley.

"Excuse me," I say and cut in. "Hey guys, can I talk to you for a moment."

"Sure," Geneva says.

"What's up?" Rhune asks.

"Oscar isn't feeling well. I'm gonna take him home. Will you guys handle things here?"

"Sure."

"Don't forget to give the return gifts. Kids table is separate."

"We'll take care of things here. Don't worry about a thing. Go take Oscar home. He needs to rest."

"Okay, thank you." I kiss Geneva's cheeks, then hug Oscar's brothers and dad.

I go in search of Rosemary and find her dancing with her son, the town sheriff, LeMarkus Vale.

"Mind if I cut in?"

"Not at all." He steps back.

"Oscar isn't feeling well. I'm going to take him home."

"Is everything alright?"

"He's having headaches. Pregnancy side effects." I shrug my shoulders.

"Anything I can do to help?"

"You have already helped us so much. I don't want to trouble you more. And I hope you love the present Oscar and I have given you."

"I love it! Very thoughtful of you guys, thank you."

I'm glad she loves it. We have asked Rosemary to become godmother to our triplets. She cried when I approached her with the godmother picture frame.

"It's no trouble at all. Now, tell me what do you need help with." She cocks her brow, her eyes probing.

I sigh and "Can you take care of things here? You can coordinate with Geneva. I have asked her to take care of giving the return gifts to the attendants."

"Yeah, sure. Don't worry about a thing here. We've got it."

"Thank you." I hug her and kiss her cheeks. "I'll see you around."

~

WE ARE LYING IN BED, snuggled under the blanket.

I'm spooning Oscar, my fingers lazily running across his belly.

"What do you think I'm carrying? A kit or a kitten?"

"A mix of both. I hope you carry at least one kit."

"Me too."

He goes silent for a beat. "I want to shift."

"Now?"

"Yeah." He nods.

"But you shifted just this morning."

"I can't explain it, but being in my animal form helps me relax. And I have less headaches and back pain."

"Is your back smarting?"

"A little."

"Okay, then shift. Do you want me to shift as well?"

"Would you?"

"Anything for you, my sweet."

We get off the bed and discard our night clothes, then lie on the carpet floor, holding each other's hand.

"Let's do this."

Oscar shuts his eyes, his chest rising as air fills his lungs. I follow him and fill my lungs with much-needed oxygen and close my eyes.

A flash, a crackling, and we both shift into our animal forms. I curl around him, my tail swishing from side to side.

I sniff his scent, and lick his fur.

Mine!

He purrs through our mating bond. *Yours!*

He lies on his back and I lick his belly.

He makes a soft sound that sounds like "muk-muk" to human ears.

He snuggles into me and sighs with contentment, and we sleep on the carpet peacefully.

Love you.

Love you too.

OSCAR

Ruhaan, Lyon, and Hiro have turned five today.

My babies have grown so much.

Ruhaan and Hiro are both their father's twin. They look just like Finnick. Salt and pepper hair, dark obsidian eyes, tanned skin, full smile.

Ruhaan and Hiro are honey badgers like their father.

Right now Ruhaan and Hiro have shifted into their animal forms and are competing to see who can dig fastest in our backyard.

In their animal forms they look so cute. And I love the gray mantle and the white stripe extending from their crown to the base of their tail.

Finnick is monitoring them, and my Lyon is checking the time.

Lyon is the oldest of the triplets. He looks like me. Honey-color hair, pale skin, and pale green eyes.

He's a bit taller than his brothers, but I'm sure Ruhaan and Hiro will catch up to him as well.

"Stop!" Lyon orders.

The boys shift back into their human form, buck-ass naked.

Finnick hands them their clothes and removes the measuring tape and checks how deep each has dug.

The boys quickly don their clothes and look at their father with large innocent eyes.

"You both have dug the same height and width. So it's a draw!"

"No!" Hiro whines.

"Again?" Ruhaan groans.

"You know you both are equal and good." Finnick musses their hair.

"But we want to see who can win!"

"Next time. Come on, your nan and poppy will be here to take you boys to the Mudworks. Off you go and take a quick shower."

The boys run inside the house like a tornado.

"Careful!"

"We are going to Mudwork, Daddy," Lyon shouts over his shoulder.

Mudworks is a make and paint or glaze your own pottery shop. My boys love visiting that place with their grandparents. It has been their birthday gift for the last two years.

After that they will come home and there will be a small party at home.

Finnick has prepared three cakes for our sons. Each one is different.

A chef in the family comes in very handy at times like these.

"Who won this round?" I ask Finnick when he climbs the porch, whispering, so the kids don't hear us.

"Hiro."

"And who won the previous round?"

"Ruhaan."

"Good of you to always come to the draw conclusion."

"They are small, they won't realize what I'm doing."

"They won't always be small."

"I know." He gives me a sad smile, then pats my swollen belly. "How are these munchkins?"

"Doing good."

"Any day now."

"Yeah, any day now."

The doorbell rings and I know it's my parents. "Help me." I lift my hands up and Finnick helps me stand, then goes to open the door.

I waddle into the house slowly, and kiss my parents on the cheek. "Hey, guys."

"How are you feeling, baby?"

"I'm feeling good, Mama."

"Don't forget we are keeping the boys with us tomorrow."

The boys will be staying with their grandparents tomorrow. It was Mama's idea to give me some time to relax.

They have a full day planned with my family tomorrow.

First they will visit the museum, then the skating rink with my brothers, then in the evening, they'll have a picnic at the Vale Valley Lake.

Everyone spoils them, dotes on them.

The boys come rushing down after fifteen minutes, all ready to have fun.

"Nan!"

"Poppy!"

The boys shout excitedly and hug my parents.

"You boys ready?"

"Yes!" they say in chorus.

I smile and wait for them to kiss us goodbye.

"Have fun, you guys." I shout as they run out.

"Listen to your nan and poppy," Finnick says, following them out.

"We will, Dada."

I sit on the sofa and rest my swollen legs on the coffee table, and close my eyes.

"Hey, sweet."

I open my eyes, my mouth curving into a small smile. "Hey."

"Legs are hurting?"

"No my back's smarting."

"Do you think you are going into labor?"

"Hard to say."

"Shall we head to the hospital?"

"Let's wait for an hour and see. If the pain intensifies then we'll go."

THE PAIN NOT ONLY INTENSIFIES, it tears me in half.

My contractions are coming fast.

We rush to the hospital, but before I can get checked in, my water breaks and I have to push.

I give birth to another set of triplets in the hospital lobby —two kittens and one kit this time.

I am then moved to a private room in the hospital, and the nurses are checking my babies vitals.

"We need to call my parents and inform them," I tell Finnick, gazing lovingly at my mate, who is gazing down at his babies with so much happiness and love as they are being cleaned by the nurses in our room.

"I already did. They will bring the boys in some time soon," he says over his shoulder.

"I feel bad for ruining their birthday party."

"They'll be happy to have three more siblings to share their birthdays with."

I laugh and shake my head. "Six kids sharing the same birth date."

"I know." He laughs as well. "Sounds so expensive!"

"Are you happy Finnick?" I pat the bed, then motion for him to come and sit with me.

He walks toward me and takes his place next to me on the bed, and wraps his arm over my shoulder. "So happy, my love."

He kisses my head and we both sigh when the babies are finally settled over my chest.

Love heals everything.

Love mends every bridge.

One meeting has changed my life, and I couldn't be happier.

I am my Chef's nutter half, and he's mine!

THE END.

THANK you for reading Chef's Nutter Half!

I hope you fell in love with Finnick and Oscar's story the way I did!

Please consider leaving a review if you have enjoyed this story. Reviews help other readers are greatly appreciated!

WANT MORE FROM THE ISHA FÁNG?" Check out her other book available.

ABOUT THE AUTHOR

Neya Wara is a wife and a mom to a three-going-on-thirty-year-old daughter. As an avid reader, she believes that everyone deserves a happily ever after. She loves sharing stories that live and come from her heart. Her characters are her soul and their world is her dream which she wishes will come true someday.

She loves writing, and some of her stories talk about her personal experience--good, bad, everything. She's always procrastinating if she's not reading. She loves to travel and explore new places. And she enjoys dancing when life permits.

Be sure not to miss new releases and sales from Neya Wara. Sign up to receive her newsletter: https://view.flodesk.-com/pages/5f8ea4d9bdb725b7d83a8688

- facebook.com/authorIshaFang
- twitter.com/NeyaWara
- goodreads.com/goodreadscomauthor_isha_fang
- bookbub.com/authors/isha-fang
- amazon.com/author/ishafang
- instagram.com/authorneyawara

REFERENCES.

1. https://www.tasteatlas.com/most-popular-desserts-in-thailand
2. https://www.weirdfacts.com/en/animal-facts/3616-fun-facts-about-honey-badgers
3. https://animals.mom.com/squirrels-make-noise-10587.html